Forbidden Dawn: A Tale of Love and Resistance in Apartheid South Africa

GPTApplied Creative Writing Group

Published by GPTApplied Press, 2024.

FORBIDDEN DAWN: A TALE OF LOVE AND RESISTANCE IN APARTHEID SOUTH AFRICA

First edition. July 4, 2024.

ISBN: 979-8227996367

Written by GPTApplied Creative Writing Group.

Table of Contents

Preface

The story you are about to read unfolds against the backdrop of one of the most challenging periods in South African history. From 1948 to 1994, the system of apartheid enforced racial segregation and white supremacy in South Africa, profoundly impacting every aspect of life in the country.

Apartheid, which means "apartness" in Afrikaans, was more than just a policy; it was a complex system of laws and practices designed to separate people based on their racial classification. This system restricted where people could live, work, and socialize, whom they could marry, and even which public facilities they could use. For the black majority, as well as other non-white groups, it meant a life of oppression, limited opportunities, and constant struggle.

However, in the face of this injustice, a powerful resistance movement emerged. This movement, comprising people from all racial backgrounds, fought tirelessly against the apartheid regime. Their methods ranged from peaceful protests and civil disobedience to underground resistance and international advocacy. The struggle was long and often dangerous, with many paying a heavy price for their involvement.

It is within this context that our story of James and Amahle takes place. While these characters are fictional, their experiences reflect the real challenges, dilemmas, and courageous choices faced by many South Africans during this tumultuous time.

As you read, you may encounter terms, events, or cultural references specific to South Africa or the apartheid era. We encourage you to view these as opportunities to deepen your understanding of this critical period in world history. The struggle against apartheid was not just a South African issue, but a global human rights concern that resonated around the world.

It's also worth noting that while apartheid officially ended in 1994 with South Africa's first democratic elections, its legacy continues to influence the country today. The journey towards true equality and reconciliation is ongoing, reflecting the complex process of healing deep societal wounds.

Our hope is that this novel not only tells a compelling story but also prompts reflection on broader themes of justice, equality, and the power of individuals to effect change. As you follow James and Amahle's journey, we invite you to consider how their experiences might relate to ongoing struggles for equality and human rights in our world today.

Thank you for joining us on this journey through a pivotal moment in history. May it inspire, challenge, and move you.

Chapter 1: Worlds Apart

The first rays of dawn crept through the small, grimy window of Amahle's room, casting long shadows across the worn floorboards. Amahle stirred, her eyes fluttering open before the shrill cry of her alarm clock could pierce the morning silence. With practiced efficiency, she silenced the clock and swung her legs over the edge of her narrow bed, allowing herself a moment to gather her thoughts before beginning another day of service.

As she dressed in her crisp uniform, Amahle's mind wandered to the dog-eared book of poetry hidden beneath her mattress. The verses of Okot p'Bitek and Léopold Sédar Senghor had been her companions through the night, their words of African pride and identity a balm to her soul. She longed to linger over them, to lose herself in the rhythm and power of their language, but such luxuries were not for a maid in the Hartley household.

Amahle moved quietly through her morning routine, careful not to wake the other servants still sleeping in the cramped quarters. As she braided her hair, her fingers moving deftly in the dim light, she allowed herself to dream. She imagined a future where she could pursue her love of literature openly, where her intelligence and passion for learning were valued rather than seen as a threat or an inconvenience.

The soft creak of a floorboard announced the arrival of Thembi, a fellow maid and Amahle's closest confidante in the household. Thembi's round face appeared in the doorway, her expression a mixture of excitement and apprehension.

"Did you hear?" Thembi whispered, her eyes darting around as if the very walls might be listening. "The young master is returning today."

Amahle nodded, securing the last pin in her hair. "Mr. James, yes. Mrs. Hartley mentioned it yesterday while I was cleaning the parlor."

Thembi moved closer, her voice dropping even lower. "They say he's been away in England, at one of those fancy universities. Do you think he'll be... different?"

Amahle paused, considering the question. She had only vague memories of James Hartley from before he left for his studies - a lanky, quiet boy who seemed more at ease among his books than with the boisterous sons of his father's friends. "I don't know, Thembi," she replied honestly. "But whatever he's like, it doesn't change things for us. We still have our duties."

Thembi's face fell slightly, the brief spark of excitement extinguished by Amahle's pragmatism. "I suppose you're right. Still, it might be nice to have a fresh face around here, even if it is just another white baas."

Amahle offered a small smile, understanding her friend's need for any break in the monotony of their lives. "We'd better get to the kitchen," she said, gathering her few belongings. "You know how Mrs. Olivier gets if breakfast is even a minute late."

As they made their way through the quiet corridors of the servants' quarters, Amahle's mind returned to the impending arrival of James Hartley. Despite her words to Thembi, she couldn't help but feel a flutter of curiosity. What changes might this educated young man bring to the carefully ordered world of the Hartley estate? And why did she feel, deep in her bones, that his return might somehow alter the course of her own carefully constrained life?

Shaking off such fanciful thoughts, Amahle straightened her shoulders and quickened her pace. There was work to be done, and dreams had no place in the harsh light of day. Yet as she pushed through the kitchen doors, ready to face another day of service, a small part of her continued to hope, continued to believe that someday, somehow, her world might expand beyond the confining walls of servitude and segregation.

THE HARTLEY FAMILY'S living room was awash in the warm glow of afternoon sunlight, filtering through the tall, ornate windows that overlooked the manicured garden. Eleanor Hartley fussed with the arrangement of fresh-cut roses in a crystal vase, while her husband, Richard, paced impatiently, occasionally glancing at his gold pocket watch.

The crunch of tires on gravel announced the arrival they'd been anticipating. Eleanor's hands fluttered to her perfectly coiffed hair as she moved to stand beside her husband. "Richard, he's here," she breathed, a mixture of excitement and apprehension in her voice.

The heavy oak door swung open, and James Hartley stepped into the room, a leather suitcase in one hand and a worn satchel slung over his shoulder. He looked older than when he'd left, his boyish features having sharpened into those of a young man. His clothes, while of obvious quality, had a rumpled, lived-in look that contrasted sharply with his parents' impeccable appearance.

"James, darling!" Eleanor rushed forward, enveloping her son in a perfumed embrace. "Welcome home."

James returned the hug somewhat stiffly, his eyes meeting his father's over his mother's shoulder. "Hello, Mother. Father."

Richard stepped forward, clasping James's hand in a firm handshake. "Good to have you back, son. The drive from Cape Town treat you well?"

James nodded, setting down his luggage. "It was fine. Long, but... illuminating."

Eleanor ushered him to the plush sofa, eager to have him sit. "You must tell us everything about Oxford. Were your studies fulfilling? Did you make many friends?"

James sank into the cushions, a slight furrow appearing between his brows. "It was... eye-opening," he said carefully. "I learned a great deal, both in and out of the classroom."

Richard settled into his armchair, reaching for his pipe. "Well, now that you're back, we must discuss your future. I've spoken with Hendrik van der Merwe about a position at the bank. It would be an excellent starting point for you."

James's posture stiffened almost imperceptibly. "Actually, Father, I've been giving a lot of thought to my future. I'm considering pursuing journalism. Perhaps even some freelance writing."

A heavy silence fell over the room. Eleanor's smile faltered, while Richard's pipe remained unlit in his hand.

"Journalism?" Richard's voice was carefully controlled. "James, surely you jest. With your education and our connections, you could have any respectable position you desire."

James leaned forward, his voice earnest. "That's just it, Father. I've seen a world beyond what we have here. There are stories that need to be told, injustices that need to be exposed."

Eleanor's hand flew to her throat. "James, darling, you're not talking about... politics, are you? You know how dangerous that can be."

"It's not about politics, Mother. It's about truth. About seeing people - all people - as they really are."

Richard's face darkened. "I see your time abroad has filled your head with idealistic nonsense. You have a responsibility to this family, to our position in society."

James stood, running a hand through his hair in frustration. "And what about our responsibility to our fellow human beings? The things I've seen since I've been back, the way people are treated... it's not right, Father."

"Enough!" Richard's voice boomed through the room. "You're tired from your journey. We'll discuss this further once you've had time to readjust to life here."

James opened his mouth as if to argue further, but then thought better of it. "Of course, Father. If you'll excuse me, I'd like to freshen up before dinner."

As James gathered his luggage and headed for the stairs, Eleanor and Richard exchanged worried glances. Their son had returned, but he was not the same young man who had left. The comfortable world they had built suddenly felt precarious, shaken by the winds of change that James had unknowingly brought home with him.

THE HARTLEY FAMILY'S library was a sanctuary of leather-bound volumes and the musty scent of old paper. Amahle moved quietly between the towering shelves, feather duster in hand, her movements practiced and efficient. She paused occasionally, allowing her fingers to brush lightly over the spines of books she longed to read but dared not touch beyond her duties.

The door creaked open, and Amahle froze, her heart racing. She wasn't supposed to be in here alone; Mrs. Hartley preferred the library to be cleaned under supervision. But as she turned, ready with an apology on her lips, she found herself face to face not with Mrs. Hartley, but with James.

He seemed equally startled by her presence, his blue eyes widening slightly. "Oh, I'm sorry," he said, his voice softer than she expected. "I didn't realize anyone was in here."

Amahle quickly lowered her gaze, remembering her place. "No, sir, I apologize. I was just finishing up. I'll leave you to your privacy."

As she moved to exit, James stepped further into the room, his eyes scanning the shelves. "Actually, I was looking for a book. Perhaps you could help me?" There was a hesitancy in his voice, as if he wasn't sure whether asking for her assistance was appropriate.

Amahle paused, surprised by the request. "Of course, sir. What book are you looking for?"

James ran a hand through his hair, a gesture that seemed both nervous and habitual. "It's a collection of African poetry. I remember seeing it here before I left for university, but I can't seem to locate it now."

Amahle's heart skipped a beat. She knew exactly which book he meant; it was one she had longingly admired during her cleaning sessions. "I believe I know the one, sir," she said, moving towards a shelf near the window. Her fingers traced the spines until she found what she was looking for, pulling out a slim volume bound in green cloth.

James's face lit up as she handed him the book. "Yes, this is it! Thank you..." he trailed off, realizing he didn't know her name.

"Amahle, sir," she supplied, her voice barely above a whisper.

"Amahle," he repeated, the name sounding foreign but pleasant on his tongue. "Thank you, Amahle." He opened the book, leafing through the pages. "Are you familiar with any of these poets?"

The question caught her off guard. It would be safer to deny any knowledge, to maintain the barrier between them. But something in James's earnest expression made her hesitate. "I... I've read some Okot p'Bitek, sir," she admitted cautiously. "His 'Song of Lawino' is quite powerful."

James's eyebrows rose in surprise and what looked like admiration. "You've read p'Bitek? That's remarkable. What did you think of his critique of colonialism?"

For a moment, Amahle forgot herself, her passion for literature overriding her caution. "I found it both heartbreaking and inspiring, sir. The way he juxtaposes traditional African values with imposed Western ideals... it resonates deeply."

As soon as the words left her mouth, Amahle realized she had overstepped. She quickly lowered her eyes, her hands tightening on the feather duster. "Forgive me, sir. I shouldn't presume to discuss such matters."

James took a step towards her, his voice gentle. "No, please, I'd love to hear more of your thoughts. It's refreshing to find someone who appreciates these works."

The air between them seemed to crackle with unspoken tension. Amahle knew she should excuse herself, return to her duties, and forget this encounter ever happened. But a part of her longed to stay, to engage in the kind of intellectual discourse she had always dreamed of.

Before she could respond, the sound of approaching footsteps in the hallway broke the spell. Amahle quickly stepped back, resuming her dusting. James reluctantly turned towards the bookshelves, the poetry book still in his hand.

Mrs. Hartley appeared in the doorway, her eyes narrowing slightly at the scene before her. "James, darling, I didn't realize you were in here. Amahle, have you finished your tasks?"

"Yes, ma'am," Amahle replied, her voice steady despite her racing heart. "I was just leaving."

As she slipped past Mrs. Hartley and out of the library, Amahle could feel James's eyes following her. She hurried down the hallway, her mind reeling from the encounter. It had lasted only moments, but she knew, with a certainty that both thrilled and terrified her, that everything had changed.

THE MIDDAY SUN BEAT down mercilessly on the dusty streets of the coastal town as Amahle made her way through the crowded marketplace. Her wicker basket, already half-full with the Hartleys' groceries, swung gently at her side. Despite the heat, she kept her pace brisk, knowing that Mrs. Hartley expected her back promptly.

As she walked, Amahle couldn't help but notice the invisible lines that divided the town. On one side of the street, white faces peered out from air-conditioned shops, while on the other, non-whites crowded into smaller, stuffier establishments. The segregation was so deeply ingrained that most people seemed not to notice it anymore. But Amahle noticed. She always noticed.

She approached Meneer Botha's general store, steeling herself for the interaction to come. Taking a deep breath, she pushed open the door, the little bell above tinkling cheerfully, at odds with the tension she felt.

"Yes?" Meneer Botha's gruff voice called out before he'd even looked up from his newspaper. When he did, his expression soured. "Oh, it's you. What do you want?"

Amahle stepped forward, her voice carefully modulated to be polite but not subservient. "Good afternoon, Meneer. Mrs. Hartley sent me to collect her order."

The shopkeeper grunted, heaving himself up from his chair. "Wait there," he instructed, pointing to a spot near the door. "Don't touch anything."

As he disappeared into the back of the store, Amahle remained still, acutely aware of the eyes of other customers upon her. A white woman clutched her handbag tighter as she passed, while a young boy openly stared until his mother tugged him away.

Meneer Botha returned with a paper-wrapped package. He placed it on the counter, deliberately keeping it just out of Amahle's reach. "That'll be five rand," he said, eyeing her suspiciously.

Amahle carefully counted out the money Mrs. Hartley had given her, placing it on the counter. As she reached for the package, the shopkeeper's hand shot out, grabbing her wrist.

"Let's see your other hand," he demanded. "Make sure you're not stealing anything."

Humiliation burned in Amahle's chest, but she complied, showing her empty hand. "I would never steal, Meneer," she said quietly, struggling to keep her voice steady.

He released her wrist with a dismissive grunt. "Can't be too careful with you people. Now get out, I have real customers to attend to."

Amahle gathered the package, tucking it safely into her basket. As she turned to leave, she caught sight of her reflection in the store window. For a moment, she saw not just herself, but the weight of generations of injustice reflected in her eyes.

Stepping back out into the harsh sunlight, Amahle took a moment to compose herself. The encounter with Meneer Botha was nothing new, nothing she hadn't experienced a hundred times before. Yet today, it stung more sharply, perhaps because of her earlier interaction with James in the library.

As she made her way back to the Hartley estate, Amahle's mind wandered to the book of African poetry. She thought of the words that spoke of dignity, of resistance, of hope. With each step, she straightened her back a little more, lifted her chin a little higher.

The town around her might be divided, the people separated by arbitrary lines, but Amahle carried within her the dream of a different world. And for now, that dream, however fragile, was enough to carry her home.

THE HARTLEY DINING room glowed with soft candlelight, casting flickering shadows across the polished mahogany table. James sat stiffly in his chair, acutely aware of the opulence surrounding him—the gleaming silver, the delicate china, the crystal glasses that caught and refracted the light. His parents, Richard and Eleanor, were seated at either end of the table, while the Van der Merwes—longtime friends and business associates of the Hartleys—occupied the other side.

Amahle moved silently around the table, refilling wine glasses and replacing empty dishes with practiced efficiency. James found his eyes drawn to her more than once, remembering their brief encounter in the library earlier that day.

"So, James," Hendrik Van der Merwe's booming voice cut through his thoughts. "Your father tells me you're considering a position at the bank. Excellent choice, my boy. It's important for men like us to maintain our positions of influence."

James set down his fork, choosing his words carefully. "Actually, Mr. Van der Merwe, I'm more interested in pursuing journalism. I believe there are important stories that need to be told in our country."

A heavy silence fell over the table. Eleanor's smile became fixed, while Richard's jaw tightened visibly.

"Journalism?" Hendrik's wife, Margaretha, tittered nervously. "But surely that's not a suitable profession for someone of your background, dear?"

James leaned forward, his voice earnest. "I've seen things, both abroad and since I've been home, that have opened my eyes. The inequality, the injustice—"

"James," Richard cut in sharply. "This is hardly appropriate dinner conversation."

But James pressed on, emboldened by the simmering frustration he'd felt since his return. "How can we sit here, enjoying this luxury, while just beyond our walls people are suffering? The apartheid system is—"

"Enough!" Richard's fist came down on the table, causing the cutlery to rattle. "I will not have you spouting this liberal nonsense in my house. The system protects us, maintains order."

"Order?" James scoffed. "Is that what you call it when human beings are treated as less than human because of the color of their skin?"

In the ensuing silence, the soft clink of Amahle setting down a dish seemed unnaturally loud. James glanced at her, noting the tension in her shoulders, the careful blankness of her expression.

Hendrik cleared his throat. "Now, now, let's not get carried away. James, my boy, you've been away for a while. You don't understand the complexities of our situation here."

"I understand enough," James retorted. "I understand that we're perpetuating a system of oppression and calling it civilization."

Eleanor's voice quavered as she attempted to diffuse the tension. "Perhaps we could discuss something else? Margaretha, how is your garden coming along this season?"

But the atmosphere remained charged. As the conversation awkwardly shifted to safer topics, James caught Amahle's eye as she leaned in to refill his water glass. For a brief moment, he saw a flicker of something—approval? Hope?—in her gaze before she quickly looked away.

The rest of the dinner passed in a blur of forced pleasantries and underlying tension. As the Van der Merwes prepared to leave, James excused himself, unable to bear the suffocating atmosphere any longer.

In the hallway, he paused, leaning against the wall and closing his eyes. The sound of quiet footsteps made him look up. Amahle was passing by with a stack of dirty dishes. Their eyes met, and in that moment, James felt a connection—a shared understanding of the injustice that permeated their world.

As Amahle disappeared into the kitchen, James straightened up, a newfound resolve settling over him. He knew now, more than ever, that he couldn't remain silent. Whatever the cost, he had to use his voice to fight against the system that kept people like Amahle oppressed. The dinner conversation had only strengthened his determination to pursue journalism and tell the stories that needed to be told.

THE MOON HUNG LOW IN the sky, casting a pale glow over the Hartley estate. In two separate rooms, worlds apart yet under the same roof, Amahle and James lay awake, their minds churning with the day's events.

In her small, sparse room in the servants' quarters, Amahle sat cross-legged on her bed, a worn book of African poetry open in her lap. Her fingers traced the lines of Okot p'Bitek's verses, but her thoughts were elsewhere.

"He asked for my opinion," she whispered to herself, still scarcely believing it. "He spoke to me as if... as if I mattered." The memory of James's earnest face in the library brought a warmth to her chest, quickly followed by a chill of reality. She shook her head, chiding herself for such foolish thoughts. "Don't be ridiculous, Amahle. He's the master's son. Nothing can ever come of it."

Yet, as she gazed out her small window at the moon, she couldn't help but wonder. What if things were different? What if the color of her skin didn't determine her worth in this world?

Across the estate, in his spacious bedroom, James paced restlessly. The dinner conversation replayed in his mind, his father's angry words echoing in his ears. He paused at his desk, picking up a photograph he'd taken during his travels – a group of children, black and white, playing together on a London street.

"How can they not see?" he muttered, running a hand through his hair in frustration. "How can they justify this... this madness?"

His thoughts drifted to Amahle, to the spark of intelligence he'd seen in her eyes as they discussed poetry. He remembered the way she'd carried herself at dinner, dignified despite the subservient role forced upon her. A wave of shame washed over him as he realized how little he knew about her life, about the lives of any of the people who worked for his family.

James moved to the window, leaning against the frame as he stared up at the moon. It was the same moon he'd gazed at in England, the same moon that shone over every corner of the world. "There has to be a way to change things," he whispered to the night sky. "There has to be."

In that moment, unknown to each other, Amahle and James shared the same sliver of hope. As they looked up at the same moon, their separate worlds felt a little less distant, a little more connected. The path ahead was uncertain, fraught with danger and societal barriers, but in the quiet of the night, anything seemed possible.

Amahle closed her book of poetry, holding it close to her chest as she lay down. James turned from the window, a new resolve settling over him as he finally sought his bed. As sleep began to claim them both, their last thoughts were of change, of justice, and of a world where the color of one's skin no longer determined their fate.

The moon continued its silent vigil, bearing witness to the first stirrings of a connection that would challenge the very foundations of their world.

Chapter 2: Bridging Worlds

The Hartley library lay silent in the depths of night, moonlight filtering through the tall windows and casting long shadows across the rows of bookshelves. Amahle moved quietly between the stacks, her fingers trailing reverently over the spines of leather-bound volumes. She paused, glancing nervously at the door before pulling a book from the shelf—a collection of works by Chinua Achebe.

With practiced stealth, she made her way to a plush armchair tucked away in a corner, barely visible from the entrance. Settling in, she opened the book, inhaling the scent of old paper and allowing herself a small smile of anticipation.

"Things Fall Apart," she whispered, losing herself in the opening lines. So engrossed was she in the story that she didn't hear the soft creak of the library door opening.

James Hartley stood frozen in the doorway, surprise etched across his features. He had come seeking solitude, unable to sleep and hoping to find comfort in the familiar embrace of books. Instead, he found Amahle, her face illuminated by a sliver of moonlight, completely absorbed in her reading.

For a moment, he considered retreating quietly, leaving her to her stolen moment of literary indulgence. But curiosity and a strange, inexplicable pull kept him rooted to the spot.

"Achebe?" he said softly, stepping into the room.

Amahle's head snapped up, her eyes wide with fear. The book tumbled from her hands as she scrambled to her feet. "Mr. James! I... I'm so sorry. I shouldn't be here. I was just—"

James held up a hand, his voice gentle. "Please, don't apologize. I'm not here to reprimand you." He moved closer, picking up the fallen book and holding it out to her. "You have excellent taste in literature."

Amahle hesitated, her hand trembling slightly as she took the book from him. "You're... not angry?"

"Angry? No." James smiled, settling into a nearby chair. "I'm intrigued. What do you think of Achebe's work?"

The tension in Amahle's shoulders eased slightly, though wariness still lingered in her eyes. "It's... powerful," she said cautiously. "The way he captures the clash between traditional Igbo culture and colonial influence... it resonates deeply."

James leaned forward, his eyes alight with interest. "Yes, exactly! Have you read 'No Longer at Ease'? The way Achebe explores the corruption that comes with colonialism is masterful."

As they spoke, the initial awkwardness began to melt away. Amahle sank back into her chair, her passion for literature overriding her caution. They discussed favorite passages, debated interpretations, and shared recommendations, their voices hushed but animated in the stillness of the night.

"You know," James said, a note of admiration in his voice, "I've never met anyone with such a comprehensive understanding of African literature. Your insights are remarkable, Amahle."

A flush crept up Amahle's neck, visible even in the dim light. "Thank you, Mr. James. I... I've always loved reading. It's like traveling to other worlds, seeing through other eyes."

"I couldn't agree more," James replied, his gaze lingering on her face. There was a moment of charged silence, filled with unspoken understanding and a growing awareness of their unusual connection.

The spell was broken by the sound of footsteps in the hallway outside. Amahle leapt to her feet, panic flashing across her face. James reacted instinctively, guiding her behind a tall bookshelf just as the door began to open.

Pressed close in the narrow space, they held their breath. James could feel the rapid beat of Amahle's heart, matching the frantic rhythm of his own. The beam of a flashlight swept across the room as a night watchman peered inside.

"Anyone there?" the gruff voice called out.

James and Amahle remained perfectly still, barely daring to breathe. After what felt like an eternity, the door closed, and the footsteps receded down the hallway.

They stayed hidden for a moment longer, the air between them thick with tension and unspoken emotions. Finally, Amahle stepped away, clutching the book to her chest like a shield.

"I should go," she whispered, her eyes downcast. "Thank you, Mr. James, for... for understanding."

James opened his mouth to respond, but the words caught in his throat. He wanted to tell her to stay, to keep talking about literature and life, but he knew the danger that posed for both of them. Instead, he managed a nod, his hands clenching at his sides to keep from reaching out to her.

Amahle hesitated at the door, her hand on the knob. For a moment, it seemed she might turn back, might say something more. The air between them crackled with unspoken words and forbidden possibilities. Then, with a soft sigh that might have been regret or resolution, she slipped out of the library.

James remained rooted to the spot, his mind reeling. The empty space where Amahle had stood seemed to pulse with her lingering presence. He ran a hand through his hair, his thoughts a turbulent mix of exhilaration and fear. What had just happened here? And more importantly, what would happen next?

He knew, with a certainty that both thrilled and terrified him, that everything had changed. The world of literature they'd shared had built a bridge between their separate realities, and crossing it would be as dangerous as it was irresistible.

THE MIDDAY SUN BEAT down mercilessly on the coastal town's main street as James made his way through the bustling crowd. He had come into town on an errand for his mother, but the unusual tension in the air quickly caught his attention. People hurried along the sidewalks, speaking in hushed tones, while others gathered in small groups, their faces etched with worry and excitement.

Suddenly, a chant rose from the direction of the town square. "Amandla! Awethu!" The words, unfamiliar to James, sent a ripple of energy through the crowd.

Curiosity piqued, James pushed his way towards the source of the commotion. As he rounded the corner, he was met with a sight that took his breath away. Hundreds of people, mostly Black and Coloured, had gathered in the square, holding homemade signs and banners. "Down with Apartheid!" one placard read. "Freedom Now!" declared another.

At the center of the crowd, standing atop a makeshift platform, a man with a powerful voice addressed the protesters. "We will no longer accept being treated as second-class citizens in our own land! We demand equality, we demand justice, we demand our human rights!"

The crowd roared in response, their collective voice a thunderous affirmation of shared struggle and hope.

James stood transfixed, his heart racing. He had read about protests in the newspapers, had discussed the growing resistance movement in hushed tones with like-minded students at Oxford. But to see it here, in his hometown, was something else entirely. The raw emotion, the palpable anger and determination in the air, made all his academic discussions seem pale and inadequate in comparison.

As he watched, a flicker of movement caught his eye. A young woman, her face partially obscured by a colorful headscarf, was weaving through the crowd, passing out leaflets. There was something familiar about her graceful movements, but before James could place it, she disappeared into the sea of bodies.

Suddenly, the atmosphere shifted. A line of police vehicles screeched into the square, sirens wailing. Officers in riot gear poured out, forming a menacing barrier between the protesters and the rest of the town.

"Disperse immediately!" a voice boomed through a megaphone. "This gathering is illegal. Return to your homes or face arrest!"

The crowd's chants grew louder in defiance. James watched in horror as the police advanced, batons raised. The first blow fell, then another, and another. Screams of pain and anger filled the air as chaos erupted.

James stood frozen, unable to comprehend the violence unfolding before him. He saw an elderly man knocked to the ground, a young woman dragged away by her hair. The acrid smell of tear gas stung his nostrils as canisters were lobbed into the crowd.

In the midst of the mayhem, James caught sight of the woman in the headscarf again. She was helping others escape, guiding them towards side streets and alleyways. For a brief moment, their eyes met across the square. James felt a jolt of recognition, but before he could react, she was gone.

As the square emptied, leaving behind only the injured and those being arrested, James stumbled away, his mind reeling. The carefully constructed worldview he had grown up with lay shattered at his feet, replaced by a harsh reality he could no longer ignore.

Making his way home, James's thoughts were a tumult of conflicting emotions. Shame at his own privileged ignorance warred with a burning desire to do something, anything, to fight against the injustice he had witnessed. And underneath it all, a nagging suspicion about the familiar woman in the crowd tugged at his consciousness.

One thing was certain: there was no going back to the way things were before. The unrest in the town square had awakened something in James, a fierce determination to stand on the right side of history, no matter the cost.

THE HEAVY OAK DOOR of Richard Hartley's study slammed shut, the sound reverberating through the house. James stood before his father's imposing mahogany desk, his hands clenched at his sides, still trembling from the adrenaline of the afternoon's events.

"What were you thinking?" Richard's voice was low and dangerous. "Being seen at that... that riot? Do you have any idea what this could do to our family's reputation?"

James took a deep breath, struggling to keep his voice steady. "It wasn't a riot, Father. It was a peaceful protest until the police arrived. The things I saw... the brutality..."

"Brutality?" Richard scoffed. "Those people were breaking the law. The police were simply maintaining order."

"Order?" James's voice rose. "Is that what you call beating unarmed civilians? Women and elderly people?"

Outside in the hallway, Amahle froze, duster in hand. She had been about to enter the study to clean, but the raised voices made her pause. Glancing around to ensure she was alone, she leaned closer to the door, her heart pounding.

Richard stood, his face flushed with anger. "You've been away too long, James. You've forgotten how things work here. These protests, these ideas of equality... they're dangerous. They threaten everything we've built."

"Maybe what we've built needs to be threatened," James shot back. "How can we justify living in luxury while others suffer? The apartheid system is cruel and unjust, and I won't stand by silently anymore."

A heavy silence fell over the room. Amahle held her breath, scarcely daring to move.

When Richard spoke again, his voice was cold and controlled. "I see your time abroad has filled your head with these radical notions. Let me be clear, James. If you continue down this path, if you insist on associating with these... agitators, I will have no choice but to cut you off. No more allowance, no inheritance, no place in this family."

James felt as if he'd been slapped. He stared at his father, searching for any sign of the man who had once taught him about fairness and integrity. "You'd disown your own son for standing up for what's right?"

"What's right?" Richard's laugh was bitter. "You're young, idealistic. You don't understand the complexities of our situation here. This system protects us, maintains our way of life."

"At what cost?" James asked quietly. "Our humanity?"

Another silence stretched between them, heavy with unspoken words and shattered illusions.

Finally, Richard sank back into his chair, suddenly looking older and weary. "Go to your room, James. We'll discuss this further when you've come to your senses."

James turned to leave, his hand on the doorknob when his father's voice stopped him.

"Remember, son. Everything you have, everything you are, is because of the life we've provided for you. Don't throw it all away for some misguided crusade."

Without responding, James yanked open the door. Amahle barely managed to step back in time, pressing herself against the wall as he stormed past, too preoccupied to notice her presence.

As the sound of James's footsteps faded, Amahle remained frozen in place, her mind reeling from what she had overheard. The young master's impassioned defense of her people, his father's threats, the stark divide between their worldviews – it was almost too much to process.

With trembling hands, she resumed her dusting, moving quietly into the study where Richard Hartley sat with his head in his hands. As she worked, stealing glances at the troubled man, Amahle felt the weight of change in the air. Something fundamental had shifted in the Hartley household, and she knew, with a mixture of hope and fear, that nothing would ever be quite the same again.

THE MOON HUNG LOW IN the sky, casting long shadows across the Hartley estate's manicured gardens. James paced nervously near the old oak tree at the far end of the property, his eyes darting frequently to the servants' quarters. He had slipped a note under Amahle's door earlier, asking her to meet him here at midnight. Now, as the appointed time approached, he questioned the wisdom of his impulsive action.

A soft rustle of fabric made him turn. Amahle emerged from the shadows, her expression a mixture of curiosity and apprehension.

"Mr. James?" she whispered, glancing around nervously. "We shouldn't be out here. If someone sees us—"

"I know, I know," James said quickly, gesturing for her to join him in the deeper shadows of the tree. "But I had to talk to you. About what happened in town today."

Amahle's eyes widened. "You were there? At the protest?"

James nodded, running a hand through his hair. "I saw everything. The crowds, the police, the violence. It was..." he trailed off, shaking his head. "I had no idea. All this time, I've been blind to what's really happening here."

Amahle remained silent, her posture tense. James looked at her imploringly. "Please, Amahle. I need to understand. What's it really like? Living under these laws, facing this kind of oppression every day?"

For a long moment, Amahle said nothing. Then, slowly, she began to speak. Her voice was low and measured, but James could hear the undercurrent of pain and anger as she described the daily indignities, the constant fear, the shattered dreams of her people.

As she spoke, James felt his heart constrict. He found himself moving closer, instinctively reaching out to comfort her. Their hands brushed, and a jolt of electricity seemed to pass between them. They both froze, suddenly aware of their proximity.

"Amahle, I—" James began, his voice husky.

"Don't," Amahle interrupted, taking a step back. "Please, Mr. James. We can't... this isn't possible."

The moonlight caught the glimmer of tears in her eyes, mirroring the ache James felt in his own chest. They stood there, separated by mere inches and an insurmountable societal chasm.

"I want to help," James said finally, his voice thick with emotion. "I can't stand by and watch this injustice continue. Not now that I truly see it."

Amahle looked at him, a mix of hope and resignation in her gaze. "Be careful, Mr. James. Speaking out, standing with us... it's dangerous. You could lose everything."

"Some things are worth the risk," James replied softly, his eyes never leaving hers.

A twig snapped in the distance, making them both jump. "I should go," Amahle whispered urgently. "We can't be seen together like this."

As she turned to leave, James caught her hand. "Amahle, wait. I... I need to see you again. To talk more. Please."

Amahle hesitated, then nodded almost imperceptibly before slipping away into the night.

James remained under the oak tree, his mind reeling and his heart racing. He knew that everything had changed—his view of the world, his place in it, and most of all, his feelings for Amahle. The path ahead was fraught with danger and uncertainty, but in that moment, under the vast African sky, James knew he could never go back to the way things were before.

THE OAKWOOD COUNTRY Club buzzed with the chatter of Port Elizabeth's white elite, their laughter mingling with the clink of crystal glasses and the soft strains of a string quartet. James Hartley tugged uncomfortably at his collar, feeling suffocated by more than just the stuffy evening air.

"James, darling!" His mother's voice cut through his thoughts. "Come, you must say hello to the Petersons. You remember their daughter, Sarah, don't you?"

Forcing a smile, James allowed himself to be steered towards a group of familiar faces. As pleasantries were exchanged, he found his attention wandering, his gaze sweeping across the opulent ballroom.

"... and of course, we had to let the gardener go," Mrs. Peterson was saying, her voice dripping with disdain. "You simply can't trust them with anything valuable. They're all thieves, you know."

James stiffened, the casual racism hitting him like a physical blow. He opened his mouth to object, but caught his father's warning glare from across the room.

"If you'll excuse me," he muttered, breaking away from the group. He made his way to the bar, desperately in need of a drink to dull the growing sense of alienation.

As he waited for the bartender, a flash of movement caught his eye. Amahle weaved through the crowd, a tray of champagne flutes balanced expertly in one hand. Their eyes met for a brief, electric moment before she quickly looked away, her face a mask of professional detachment.

James felt his heart race. He wanted to go to her, to speak to her as he had in the library and under the oak tree. But here, surrounded by the very people who upheld the system that kept them apart, he knew it was impossible.

"Whiskey, neat," he told the bartender, his voice rougher than he intended.

As he sipped his drink, James overheard snippets of conversation from nearby groups. Talk of business deals and social engagements was interspersed with derogatory comments about "the blacks" and their "unreasonable demands" for equality.

Each word felt like a knife twisting in his gut. How had he never noticed this before? Had he been so blind, so complicit in his privilege?

"James!" His father's booming voice interrupted his brooding. "Come here, son. Mr. Van der Merwe wants to discuss a potential position for you at the bank."

Reluctantly, James made his way over. As Mr. Van der Merwe launched into a monologue about the importance of "maintaining our way of life," James found his attention drawn once again to Amahle.

She was at the edge of the room, refilling a glass for one of the guests. The man's hand lingered too long as he took the glass, his leering gaze making James's blood boil.

Without thinking, he excused himself and strode towards them. "Is everything alright here?" he asked, his voice tight with barely controlled anger.

The man looked up, startled. "Of course, young Hartley. Just enjoying the excellent service." He winked conspiratorially.

James felt sick. "I believe this young lady has other duties to attend to," he said coldly, gesturing for Amahle to leave.

She hesitated for a moment, her eyes meeting his in a look of mingled gratitude and warning before hurrying away.

"James?" His father's voice, dangerously low, came from behind him. "A word, please."

As he turned to face his father's fury, James knew the evening was far from over. The weight of his growing convictions pressed heavily upon him, threatening to shatter the gilded world he had always known.

THE MOON HUNG HEAVY in the sky, casting long shadows across the Hartley estate. In two separate rooms, worlds apart yet under the same roof, James and Amahle lay awake, their minds churning with the events of the day.

James paced his spacious bedroom, unable to shake the disgust he felt at the country club event. The casual racism, the entitled attitudes, the way Amahle had been treated – it all swirled in his mind, stoking a fire of rebellion within him. He paused at his desk, fingering a business card he'd secretly obtained at the protest. The words "Anti-Apartheid Movement" were printed in bold letters.

Taking a deep breath, James made his decision. He would contact them tomorrow, offer his support, his voice, whatever he could give to the cause. The consequences – his father's anger, potential disinheritance, social ostracization – paled in comparison to the injustice he could no longer ignore.

Across the estate, in her small servant's quarters, Amahle sat cross-legged on her bed, a worn journal open before her. She wrote feverishly, pouring out her conflicted emotions. James's kindness at the country club had touched her deeply, but it also terrified her. To hope for more, to allow herself to feel anything for the son of her employers, could only lead to heartbreak – or worse.

Yet, as she wrote, Amahle found her resolve strengthening. She had always been careful, always played it safe. But seeing James at the protest, hearing his words of support, made her wonder if it was time to take a stand. The resistance movement was growing, and they needed every voice they could get.

As the night deepened, both James and Amahle came to their decisions. They would fight for change, each in their own way, regardless of the cost. And though they didn't know it yet, their paths were destined to intertwine in ways that would challenge everything they thought they knew about love, loyalty, and the fight for justice.

They both looked up at the moon, a silent witness to their private revolutions. Tomorrow would bring new challenges, new dangers, but also new hope. For now, in the quiet of the night, anything seemed possible.

Chapter 3: Lines Drawn

The sun had barely risen over Port Elizabeth when James slipped out of the Hartley estate, his heart pounding with a mixture of excitement and trepidation. He'd memorized the address scrawled on the back of the business card, a nondescript building in a part of town he'd rarely visited.

As he approached, James hesitated, suddenly aware of how out of place he looked in his pressed shirt and polished shoes. Taking a deep breath, he pushed open the door and stepped into a world he'd only glimpsed from afar.

The headquarters of the local anti-apartheid movement was a hive of activity, even at this early hour. Posters advocating for equality and justice covered the walls, while a group of people huddled around a large table, poring over maps and documents.

A tall, stern-looking woman approached him, her eyes narrowing with suspicion. "Can I help you?"

James swallowed hard, finding his voice. "I... I want to help. With the movement."

The woman, who introduced herself as Thandi, regarded him skeptically. "And why should we trust you, rich boy? How do we know you're not a spy?"

Before James could respond, a familiar voice cut through the tension. "He was at the protest. I saw him."

James turned to see the woman he'd glimpsed distributing leaflets, her headscarf now absent. With a jolt, he realized it was Nomsa, one of the Hartley's former maids who'd been dismissed last year.

Nomsa stepped forward, her gaze challenging as she addressed James. "Why are you here, really?"

James met her eyes, his resolve strengthening. "Because I can't unsee what I've seen. The injustice, the cruelty of the system... I want to fight against it. I have resources, connections. I want to use them for the cause."

A tense silence followed his declaration. Finally, Thandi nodded. "Very well. But understand this – if you're with us, you're all in. There's no middle ground in this fight."

As James was led deeper into the building, introduced to key members and briefed on their strategies, the gravity of his decision began to sink in. He learned of planned protests, underground networks helping people escape persecution, and covert operations to expose government brutality.

With each revelation, James felt a mix of admiration for these brave individuals and a growing unease about the dangers they faced. The consequences of discovery loomed large in his mind – imprisonment, torture, or worse.

As the meeting concluded, Thandi pulled James aside. "We'll be in touch with your first assignment. Remember, trust no one outside this room. The walls have ears, especially in your world."

James nodded, his mind reeling. As he stepped back out into the morning light, he felt irrevocably changed. The path ahead was fraught with peril, but he knew there was no turning back. He was now a part of something much bigger than himself, a fight for justice that would reshape his world in ways he could scarcely imagine.

THE MIDDAY SUN STREAMED through the windows of the Hartley mansion, casting long shadows across the polished floors. Amahle moved quietly through the parlor, dusting ornate picture frames with practiced efficiency. Her mind, however, was far from her task, dwelling on the secret meetings with James and the growing unrest in the city.

"Amahle!" Mrs. Hartley's sharp voice cut through her reverie. "I've been calling you for ages. Where is your head today?"

Amahle straightened, forcing her face into a mask of calm deference. "I'm sorry, ma'am. I didn't hear you. How can I help?"

Eleanor Hartley's eyes narrowed, scrutinizing Amahle with barely concealed suspicion. "The silver needs polishing before tonight's dinner party. And do be more attentive. I won't tolerate daydreaming."

"Yes, ma'am. Right away," Amahle replied, moving towards the door.

"One more thing," Mrs. Hartley added, her tone deceptively casual. "Have you noticed anything... unusual about James lately? He seems distracted."

Amahle's heart raced, but she kept her expression neutral. "No, ma'am. Nothing unusual."

As she turned to leave, James entered the room, his presence immediately filling the space. "Mother, I heard you calling. Is everything alright?"

Eleanor's demeanor softened slightly. "Ah, James. Yes, I was just reminding Amahle of her duties. She seems rather absent-minded lately."

James's eyes flickered to Amahle, a hint of concern visible only to her. "I'm sure Amahle is doing her best, Mother. The household couldn't run without her capable assistance."

The unexpected praise hung in the air, causing Eleanor's brow to furrow. "Well, yes, I suppose. Amahle, you may go now."

As Amahle hurried from the room, she could feel Mrs. Hartley's gaze boring into her back. Behind her, she heard the conversation continue in hushed tones.

"James, darling, I hope you're not getting too... familiar with the staff. It's not appropriate for someone of your standing."

"Mother, please. Amahle is a hardworking member of this household. She deserves our respect."

"Respect is one thing, James. But don't forget your place – or hers."

The words faded as Amahle reached the kitchen, her hands trembling slightly as she gathered the silver polish. She knew the dangers of her secret meetings with James, but hearing Mrs. Hartley's suspicions voiced so plainly sent a chill through her.

As she began her task, Amahle couldn't shake the feeling that she was being watched. Glancing up, she caught sight of Thomas, one of the newer household staff, quickly averting his gaze. A seed of doubt planted itself in her mind. Could there be an informant among the staff?

The afternoon wore on, thick with unspoken tensions and growing suspicions. Amahle moved through her tasks mechanically, her mind racing with the implications of discovery. As the sun began to set, casting long shadows across the manicured lawn, she knew that the delicate balance they had maintained was shifting. Lines were being drawn, and soon, there would be no middle ground left to stand on.

THE MOON HUNG LOW IN the sky, casting long shadows across the Hartley estate. In a secluded corner of the garden, hidden from view by a dense row of hedges, James and Amahle sat huddled together on a weathered stone bench.

"'To be or not to be, that is the question,'" James read softly, his finger tracing the lines in the worn copy of Shakespeare's Hamlet. "What do you think Hamlet means by this, Amahle?"

Amahle's brow furrowed in concentration, her eyes fixed on the page. "He's... questioning his existence? Whether it's better to live or die?"

James nodded encouragingly. "Exactly. He's grappling with the weight of his choices and their consequences. Much like we are now, in a way."

Their eyes met, a moment of shared understanding passing between them. Amahle looked away first, her voice barely above a whisper. "It's dangerous, what we're doing. If we're caught..."

"I know," James replied, his hand instinctively moving to cover hers before he caught himself. "But education, knowledge – these are powerful weapons against oppression. You deserve this opportunity, Amahle."

She smiled softly, turning back to the book. As they continued reading, discussing the themes of justice, morality, and power in Hamlet, their voices blended in the night air, creating a bubble of intellectual intimacy that seemed to exist outside the harsh realities of their world.

Suddenly, a twig snapped nearby. They froze, eyes wide with alarm. James quickly stuffed the book into his jacket as Amahle stood, smoothing her apron with trembling hands.

"Who's there?" James called out, trying to keep his voice steady.

A figure emerged from the shadows – Thomas, the new gardener. His eyes darted between James and Amahle, a mixture of confusion and suspicion on his face.

"Forgive me, Mr. James," Thomas said, his voice carefully neutral. "I was just doing a final check of the grounds. I didn't realize anyone was out here."

James straightened, adopting the authoritative tone he'd heard his father use countless times. "No need to apologize, Thomas. Amahle was just helping me locate a book I'd misplaced earlier. We're finished now."

Amahle nodded, keeping her eyes downcast. "Good night, Mr. James. Thomas." She hurried away, her heart pounding in her chest.

As James watched her go, he couldn't shake the feeling that their secret meetings were becoming increasingly perilous. The world was closing in around them, and soon, they would have to face the consequences of their actions.

Thomas lingered for a moment, his gaze inscrutable. "Will that be all, sir?"

"Yes, thank you, Thomas," James replied, fighting to keep his voice even. As he made his way back to the house, the weight of Shakespeare's words echoed in his mind. To be or not to be – to fight or to conform. The question hung in the air, unanswered and heavy with implications.

THE HEAVY OAK DOOR of Richard Hartley's study closed with a resounding thud, sealing James inside with his father. The room, usually a sanctuary of quiet contemplation, crackled with tension.

Richard stood behind his desk, his face a mask of barely contained fury. "Sit down, James," he commanded, his voice low and dangerous.

James remained standing, his heart racing but his resolve firm. "I'd prefer to stand, Father."

Richard's eyes narrowed. "Very well. Do you know why I've called you here?"

"I can guess," James replied, his tone carefully neutral.

"Can you?" Richard's voice rose sharply. "Can you guess the embarrassment, the shame you've brought upon this family? Consorting with agitators, attending illegal gatherings—"

"They're not illegal, Father," James interrupted. "They're people fighting for their basic human rights."

Richard slammed his fist on the desk, causing James to flinch. "Enough! I've had reports of you seen at that... that den of radicals in town. Do you have any idea what this could do to our reputation, our standing in the community?"

James took a deep breath, steeling himself. "Maybe our standing needs to change. The system is unjust, Father. How can we continue to benefit from the oppression of others?"

Richard's face flushed deep red. "Benefit? Everything we have, we've earned. I've worked hard to provide for this family, to give you opportunities—"

"Opportunities denied to others based solely on the color of their skin," James countered.

A heavy silence fell between them. Richard moved around the desk, his voice dropping to a dangerous whisper. "Listen to me very carefully, James. This ends now. You will cease all contact with these rabble-rousers. You will take the position at the bank that Mr. Van der Merwe has so generously offered. You will behave as befits your station."

James met his father's gaze, his voice steady. "And if I refuse?"

Richard's eyes hardened. "Then you leave me no choice. You will be cut off. No more allowance, no inheritance, no place in this family. Is that what you want? To throw away everything for some misguided idealism?"

The weight of the ultimatum hung in the air between them. James felt the full force of his father's expectations, the pressure of generations of privilege bearing down upon him. For a moment, he wavered, the fear of losing everything he'd ever known threatening to overwhelm his newfound convictions.

But then he thought of Amahle, of the brave men and women he'd met at the resistance headquarters, of the injustices he could no longer ignore. His voice, when he spoke, was quiet but firm.

"I'm sorry, Father. But I can't be part of this system anymore. I have to follow my conscience."

Richard's face hardened, all trace of fatherly affection vanishing. "Then you've made your choice. Pack your things. I want you out of this house by morning."

As James turned to leave, his hand on the doorknob, Richard's voice stopped him. "Remember this moment, James. Remember that you chose to turn your back on your family, on everything we've built."

James paused, looking back at his father one last time. "No, Father. I'm choosing to stand for something greater than just our family. I hope one day you'll understand."

With that, he stepped out of the study, closing the door softly behind him. The sound echoed through the hallway, marking the end of one chapter of his life and the uncertain beginning of another.

THE AIR IN THE SMALL, dimly lit room was thick with tension and the acrid smell of cigarette smoke. Amahle sat nervously on a rickety chair, her eyes darting between the faces of the dozen or so people gathered in the cramped space. This was her first time attending an underground resistance meeting, and the gravity of the situation weighed heavily on her.

A tall, broad-shouldered man named Sipho cleared his throat, bringing the murmured conversations to a halt. "Thank you all for coming," he began, his voice low but commanding.

"We have new information about police movements in the township. Amahle?"

All eyes turned to her, and Amahle felt her heart race. Taking a deep breath, she stood, willing her voice not to shake. "The Hartleys were discussing a planned raid at their dinner party. It's set for next week, Tuesday night. They're targeting the eastern section of the township."

A ripple of concern spread through the room. Sipho nodded grimly. "This information could save lives. Thank you, Amahle."

As the meeting continued, plans were made to warn residents and prepare safe houses. Amahle listened intently, her mind reeling at the scope and complexity of the resistance network. She had always known of its existence, but being here, in the heart of it, made everything so much more real – and dangerous.

Suddenly, a heated argument broke out between two members. "We can't just keep reacting!" a young man shouted. "We need to take the fight to them!"

"And risk everything we've built?" an older woman countered. "We must be strategic, patient."

As the debate raged on, Amahle found herself thinking of the Hartleys – of Mrs. Hartley's suspicious glances, of Mr. Hartley's stern authority, and of James. Sweet, idealistic James, who was risking everything to fight for what he believed in.

A cold realization washed over her. If the resistance escalated their actions, the Hartleys could be targets. James could be in danger. The two worlds she straddled were colliding, and she was caught in the middle.

As the meeting drew to a close, Sipho approached Amahle. "You've taken a great risk coming here," he said softly. "Are you sure you're prepared for what may come?"

Amahle met his gaze, her voice steadier than she felt. "I have to be. We all do."

Leaving the meeting, Amahle stepped into the cool night air, her mind churning with conflicting emotions. She had taken a decisive step into the struggle, but at what cost? As she made her way back to the Hartley estate, the weight of her choices pressed down upon her, and she knew that there was no turning back now.

THE MOON CAST LONG shadows across the Hartley estate, its pale light illuminating two figures in separate rooms, each grappling with the weight of their decisions.

In his spacious bedroom, James sat at his desk, pen hovering over a blank sheet of paper. The events of the day - his father's ultimatum, the realization that he could lose everything - weighed heavily on his mind. With a deep breath, he began to write:

"Dear Mother and Father,

By the time you read this, I will have left. I cannot in good conscience continue to benefit from a system that oppresses and dehumanizes others. I understand that my choice may be incomprehensible to you, but I hope that one day you will see that it comes from a place of love - not just for our family, but for all of humanity..."

Across the estate, in her small servant's quarters, Amahle paced the narrow confines of her room. The clandestine meeting had opened her eyes to the true scope of the resistance, and the dangers that came with it. She paused at her meager bookshelf, running her fingers over the spines of the books James had given her.

With sudden resolve, she pulled out a worn notebook and began to write, documenting everything she had learned - names, dates, plans. If she was going to commit to this fight, she would do so fully, using every tool at her disposal.

As the night deepened, both James and Amahle came to their decisions. James sealed his letter, packing a small bag with only the essentials. Amahle tucked her notebook into a hidden pocket of her dress, her jaw set with determination.

When dawn broke, it would find them both changed - James, no longer the privileged son of the Hartley estate, but a man willing to sacrifice everything for his principles; Amahle, no longer just a maid with secret aspirations, but an active participant in the fight for justice.

The sun rose on a new day, full of uncertainty and danger, but also hope. For James and Amahle, there was no turning back now. The moment of truth had arrived, and they had chosen their paths.

Chapter 4: Worlds Colliding

The first light of dawn was just beginning to streak the sky as James Hartley stood in his bedroom, a small suitcase at his feet. He cast a final glance around the room that had been his sanctuary for so many years, now feeling more like a gilded cage. With a deep breath, he picked up his bag and the sealed letter he'd written to his parents, and stepped out into the hallway.

The house was quiet, but not entirely still. As James made his way down the grand staircase, he saw Mrs. Zulu, the elderly housekeeper, emerge from the kitchen. Her eyes widened at the sight of him with his suitcase.

"Mr. James," she whispered, her voice a mixture of concern and understanding. "You're leaving?"

James nodded, setting his bag down to embrace the woman who had been more of a mother to him than his own at times. "I have to, Mrs. Zulu. I can't stay here and pretend anymore."

Mrs. Zulu patted his cheek, her eyes glistening. "I understand, my boy. You have a good heart. Be safe out there."

As James reached for the front door, a voice from behind stopped him cold. "James? What's the meaning of this?"

He turned to see his mother, Eleanor, standing at the foot of the stairs in her dressing gown, her face a mask of confusion and growing alarm.

"I'm leaving, Mother," James said, his voice steady despite the turmoil in his heart. "Father made his position clear last night. I can't live under his rules anymore."

Eleanor rushed forward, grabbing James's arm. "Don't be ridiculous, darling. Your father was upset, but he didn't mean... You can't possibly be serious about this!"

James gently removed his mother's hand, pressing the letter into it instead. "I am serious, Mother. I've made my decision. Please, try to understand."

"Understand?" Eleanor's voice rose, tinged with hysteria. "Understand that my son is throwing away everything we've given him? Everything we've worked for?"

"No," James replied, his resolve strengthening. "Understand that I'm fighting for something bigger than just our family. For justice, for equality."

Eleanor's face crumpled, tears spilling down her cheeks. "Please, James. Don't do this. We can talk to your father, make him see reason."

For a moment, James wavered. The sight of his mother's distress, the thought of leaving behind everything he'd ever known – it almost overwhelmed him. But then he thought of Amahle, of the brave men and women he'd met in the resistance, of the injustices he could no longer ignore.

"I'm sorry, Mother," he said softly, leaning in to kiss her cheek. "I love you, but I have to do this. I hope someday you'll understand."

With that, James picked up his suitcase and stepped out into the cool morning air. As he walked down the long driveway, away from the only home he'd ever known, he could hear his mother's muffled sobs fading behind him.

The sun was rising fully now, casting long shadows across the manicured lawns of the Hartley estate. James didn't look back as he reached the gates, his steps growing more confident with each moment. He was leaving behind a world of privilege and comfort, stepping into an uncertain future. But for the first time in his life, he felt truly free.

THE SMALL ROOM BUZZED with hushed voices and nervous energy as Amahle slipped through the door, her heart pounding. This wasn't her first resistance meeting, but it was the first time she'd been asked to take a more active role. The faces around her were familiar now – Sipho, the de facto leader; Nomsa, fierce and determined; and a dozen others, all risking everything for the cause.

Sipho's deep voice cut through the murmurs. "Quiet, everyone. We have important matters to discuss." His eyes found Amahle, and he nodded for her to step forward. "Amahle has new information for us."

Taking a deep breath, Amahle moved to the center of the room. She could feel the weight of expectation on her shoulders. "There's going to be a raid," she began, her voice steadier than she felt. "Next Thursday. They're targeting the western section of the township."

A ripple of concern spread through the group. Nomsa leaned forward, her eyes sharp. "How do you know this?"

"I overheard Mr. Hartley discussing it with the police chief," Amahle replied. "They think there's a weapons cache hidden there."

Sipho's brow furrowed. "This is valuable information, Amahle. Thank you." He turned to the group. "We need to warn the residents, set up safe houses. Nomsa, can you handle that?"

As the meeting progressed, plans were made and tasks assigned. Amahle found herself at the heart of it all, providing details about police movements and the Hartleys' connections. With each piece of information she shared, she felt a mix of pride and fear. She was making a difference, but at what cost?

As the meeting drew to a close, Sipho pulled Amahle aside. "You're taking on a lot of risk," he said softly. "Are you sure you're prepared for this?"

Amahle thought of James, of his courage in leaving everything behind. She thought of the daily indignities she and her people faced. Her jaw set with determination. "I have to be," she replied. "We all do."

Sipho nodded, a hint of admiration in his eyes. "Be careful, Amahle. The more involved you become, the more dangerous it gets."

As she made her way back to the Hartley estate in the growing dusk, Amahle's mind raced. She was no longer just a maid with secret aspirations. She was an active participant in the fight for justice. The thought both thrilled and terrified her.

Approaching the grand house, Amahle paused, looking up at the lit windows. Inside was a world of privilege built on the backs of her people. And somewhere out there was James, fighting the same battle from a different angle.

With a deep breath, Amahle straightened her uniform and entered the house. She had chosen her path, and there was no turning back now. Whatever came next, she would face it with the strength and determination of those who had come before her, fighting for a better future.

THE SMALL APARTMENT was a far cry from the opulent Hartley estate. James stood in the center of the sparse living room, surrounded by peeling wallpaper and the faint smell of mildew. This was his new home, a modest flat in a mixed-race area of Port Elizabeth.

As he unpacked his meager belongings, the reality of his decision began to sink in. The worn sofa, the tiny kitchenette, the creaky bed – it was all so different from the life he'd left behind. But with each item he placed, James felt a strange mix of trepidation and liberation.

A knock at the door startled him. Opening it, he found himself face to face with his new neighbor, a middle-aged Coloured man with kind eyes.

"Welcome to the building," the man said, extending his hand. "I'm David."

James shook it, noting the momentary surprise in David's eyes at his firm grip. "James. Nice to meet you."

As they chatted, James became acutely aware of the subtle ways David's manner changed – a slight hesitation before speaking, a careful choice of words. It was a dance James had seen countless times before, but always from the other side.

Later that afternoon, James made his way to the offices of "The Truth Seeker," the anti-apartheid newspaper that had agreed to take him on. The small, cluttered space hummed with activity. As he entered, conversations halted, and all eyes turned to him.

The editor, a gruff man named Marcus, approached. "Ah, the Hartley boy. Come to slum it with us common folk?"

James felt his face flush. "I'm here to work, to make a difference."

Marcus's eyes softened slightly. "We'll see about that. For now, you can start by sorting through these tip-line calls. Learn to separate the wheat from the chaff."

As James settled into his tiny desk, he could feel the wary glances of his coworkers. He was an outsider here, his privileged background a barrier he'd have to overcome.

Hours later, as the sun began to set, James made his way back to his apartment. The streets were different here – more crowded, less manicured. He passed a group of young men who eyed him suspiciously, muttering among themselves.

Inside his flat, James sank onto the worn sofa, the events of the day washing over him. He thought of his family, of the comfort he'd left behind. But most of all, he thought of Amahle. Had he done the right thing, leaving her behind at the estate? Was she safe?

As night fell over Port Elizabeth, James stared out his grimy window at the unfamiliar skyline. He had chosen this path, this new life. It would be hard, he knew, but as he thought of the stories he'd read today, the injustices he was now positioned to expose, he felt a renewed sense of purpose.

Tomorrow would bring new challenges, new prejudices to overcome. But for now, in the quiet of his small apartment, James allowed himself to feel a glimmer of hope. He was where he needed to be, doing what he knew was right. And that, he decided, was worth any hardship he might face.

THE SUN BEAT DOWN MERCILESSLY on the streets of Port Elizabeth as a sea of people moved forward, their voices raised in unified chants for justice and equality. James found himself swept along with the crowd, his heart pounding with a mixture of excitement and apprehension. This was his first time participating in a protest since leaving home, and the energy was palpable.

"Amandla!" a voice called out. "Awethu!" the crowd responded thunderously.

James joined in, his voice blending with the others. He clutched his press badge tightly, ready to document whatever unfolded. As they rounded a corner, the atmosphere suddenly shifted. A line of police vehicles blocked the road ahead, officers in riot gear forming an ominous barrier.

A tense silence fell over the crowd. James could feel the collective intake of breath, the moment suspended between peace and chaos. Then, without warning, it shattered.

"Disperse immediately!" a voice boomed through a megaphone. "This gathering is illegal!"

Before anyone could react, the sharp crack of tear gas canisters filled the air. Panic erupted as acrid smoke billowed through the crowd. James's eyes burned, his lungs screaming for clean air. Through the haze, he saw police advancing, batons swinging indiscriminately.

Amidst the chaos, a familiar figure caught his eye. Amahle, her face partially covered by a scarf, was helping an elderly woman away from the fray. Their eyes met for a brief moment, a flash of recognition and shared purpose, before she disappeared into the crowd.

James raised his camera, determined to capture the brutality unfolding before him. He saw a young boy knocked to the ground, a woman's anguished cry as she was dragged away. Each click of the shutter felt like a small act of defiance against the injustice.

Suddenly, a hand gripped his arm. "Move!" a gruff voice shouted. James turned to see David, his neighbor, pulling him away from an advancing officer. They ran together, ducking into a narrow alley to catch their breath.

"Thank you," James gasped, his eyes still stinging from the tear gas.

David nodded grimly. "Welcome to the struggle, my friend. This is what we're up against."

As the sounds of the protest faded, replaced by distant sirens and shouts, James leaned against the cool brick wall. The weight of what he'd witnessed settled over him. This wasn't just a story to report; it was a battle for human dignity, and he was now irrevocably part of it.

With shaking hands, James checked his camera, ensuring the precious film was intact. These images would tell the truth that the government tried to suppress. As he and David cautiously made their way back to their neighborhood, James's resolve strengthened. He had seen the face of oppression up close, and he knew now more than ever that he had made the right choice in joining the fight against it.

MR. HARTLEY'S STUDY was bathed in the warm glow of the afternoon sun as he sat at his imposing mahogany desk, rifling through a stack of papers. His brow furrowed as he reached for a leather-bound notebook that had fallen behind the desk. Opening it absently, his eyes suddenly widened in shock.

"Eleanor!" he bellowed, his face flushing with anger. "Call Amahle in here immediately!"

Moments later, Amahle stood before Mr. Hartley, her heart racing but her face a mask of calm. "You wanted to see me, sir?"

Mr. Hartley held up the notebook, his voice dangerously low. "Would you care to explain this?"

Amahle's blood ran cold as she recognized her resistance notebook. She must have dropped it during her last cleaning of the study. "I... I don't know what that is, sir," she stammered.

"Don't lie to me!" Mr. Hartley exploded, slamming the book on the desk. "This is filled with information about police movements, protest plans. You've been spying on us, haven't you?"

Amahle stood frozen, her mind racing. Should she deny everything? Try to run? The weight of her choices pressed down upon her as she realized the gravity of her situation.

"Answer me!" Mr. Hartley demanded, rising from his chair.

In that moment, Amahle made her decision. Squaring her shoulders, she met Mr. Hartley's gaze. "Yes, sir. I have been gathering information for the resistance. Because it's the right thing to do."

The silence that followed was deafening. Mr. Hartley's face contorted with a mix of anger and disbelief. "You ungrateful... after everything we've done for you!"

"Done for me?" Amahle's voice rose, years of pent-up frustration breaking through. "You've kept me in servitude, denied me basic rights, all while benefiting from an unjust system."

Mr. Hartley reached for the telephone. "I'm calling the police. You'll rot in jail for this."

Amahle's heart pounded, but she stood her ground. "Go ahead. I'm not ashamed of fighting for justice."

As Mr. Hartley dialed, Amahle knew her life at the estate was over. But a strange sense of calm washed over her. Whatever came next, she would face it with the strength of her convictions.

THE SAFE HOUSE WAS a hive of activity, resistance members hurriedly preparing for the next day's operation. James stood near the back, still feeling like an outsider despite weeks of working with the movement. Suddenly, a commotion at the door caught his attention.

"We've got another one," a voice called out. "From the Hartley estate."

James's heart stopped as he saw Amahle being ushered in, looking shaken but determined. Their eyes met across the crowded room, a moment of shared shock and recognition.

"Amahle?" James breathed, pushing through the crowd towards her. "What happened?"

Amahle's eyes widened. "James? I... Mr. Hartley found my notebook. I had to run."

The room fell silent, all eyes on the unexpected reunion. Sipho stepped forward, his gaze sharp. "You two know each other?"

James nodded, suddenly aware of the tension. "Amahle worked for my family. I... I left to join the resistance."

Murmurs rippled through the group. Amahle straightened, her voice steady. "James is trustworthy. He's been fighting for our cause."

A heavy silence fell. Finally, Sipho spoke. "We'll discuss this later. For now, we need to focus on keeping Amahle safe and continuing our work."

As the others returned to their tasks, James and Amahle found a quiet corner. The air between them crackled with unspoken words and shared struggles.

"I'm sorry," James said softly. "I should have done more to protect you."

Amahle shook her head. "We both made our choices, James. Now we're here, fighting together."

Their eyes met, months of repressed feelings bubbling to the surface. In that moment, despite the danger surrounding them, a spark of hope ignited. They were no longer separated by the barriers of their past. Here, in the heart of the resistance, their paths had finally converged.

As the night wore on, James and Amahle worked side by side, their shared purpose stronger than ever. Whatever challenges lay ahead, they would face them together, united in their fight for justice and equality.

Chapter 5: The Storm Breaks

The air in the safehouse was thick with tension, a palpable unease that seemed to seep from the peeling wallpaper and creaky floorboards. James stood near the window, his back pressed against the wall, acutely aware of the suspicious glances thrown his way. The room was crowded with resistance members, their hushed conversations punctuated by occasional outbursts of heated debate.

Sipho's deep voice cut through the murmurs. "Quiet, everyone. We need to discuss our newest... situation." His eyes fixed on James, a mix of wariness and curiosity in his gaze.

A young man named Themba stepped forward, his face twisted with anger. "Why is he even here? How do we know he's not a spy?"

James opened his mouth to defend himself, but Amahle beat him to it. She moved to stand beside him, her chin raised defiantly. "James has proven himself. He left everything behind to join our cause."

Themba scoffed. "Left everything? You mean his mansion and servants? How convenient that he shows up just as things are heating up."

The room erupted into arguments, voices rising as people took sides. James felt a knot forming in his stomach. He had expected some resistance, but the depth of mistrust was overwhelming.

"Enough!" Sipho's voice boomed, silencing the room. He turned to James, his expression unreadable. "James, I need to know. Are you truly committed to this fight? Even if it means going against your own family?"

James met Sipho's gaze, his voice steady despite his racing heart. "I am. I've seen the injustice, the cruelty of the system. I can't go back to ignoring it, no matter the cost."

A tense silence followed his words. Amahle's hand found his, a small gesture of support that didn't go unnoticed by the others.

Nomsa, one of the older members, spoke up. "I say we give him a chance. We need all the help we can get, especially someone with inside knowledge of the Hartleys' circle."

Murmurs of agreement and dissent rippled through the room. Sipho held up his hand, silencing them once more. "We'll put it to a vote. Those in favor of allowing James to remain and work with us?"

Hands raised slowly, some confident, others hesitant. James held his breath as Sipho counted.

"It's decided then," Sipho announced after a moment. "James stays. But," he added, his eyes narrowing, "he'll be watched closely. Any sign of betrayal, and he's out. Understood?"

James nodded solemnly. "Understood. Thank you for this chance. I won't let you down."

As the meeting broke up, James could feel the weight of expectation and suspicion on his shoulders. Amahle squeezed his hand, offering a small smile of encouragement.

"It won't be easy," she whispered. "But we're in this together now."

James nodded, his resolve strengthening despite the challenges ahead. He had chosen this path, and he would see it through, no matter the cost. The safehouse may be filled with tension, but it was also filled with hope – hope for a better future, a just society. And that, James knew, was worth fighting for.

THE MORNING SUN STREAMED through the tall windows of the Hartley estate, casting long shadows across the polished floors. The house was unnaturally quiet, a stark contrast to the turmoil brewing within its walls.

Richard Hartley sat at the head of the dining table, his breakfast untouched before him. His wife, Eleanor, paced the length of the room, her usually perfectly coiffed hair disheveled from running her hands through it repeatedly.

"How could this happen, Richard?" Eleanor's voice was strained, barely above a whisper. "First James, and now... Amahle?"

Richard's jaw clenched at the mention of their son's name. "They've poisoned his mind with their radical ideas. And Amahle..." He slammed his fist on the table, causing the china to rattle. "That ungrateful girl. After everything we've done for her."

A sharp knock at the door interrupted their conversation. Williams, the butler, entered, his face grave. "Sir, there are police officers here to see you."

Eleanor's hand flew to her throat. "Police? What could they want?"

Richard stood, straightening his jacket. "Show them in, Williams. And bring some coffee."

Moments later, two stern-faced officers entered the dining room. The older of the two, a Captain Viljoen, spoke first. "Mr. and Mrs. Hartley, we need to ask you some questions about your son, James, and your former maid, Amahle Ndlovu."

Eleanor sank into a chair, her face pale. "Our James has nothing to do with... with whatever that girl has done."

Captain Viljoen's eyebrow raised slightly. "We have reason to believe your son has been involved with anti-government activities. And the notebook found in your study suggests Ms. Ndlovu was gathering sensitive information. We need to know everything you know about their activities and whereabouts."

Richard's face flushed with anger and embarrassment. "This is preposterous. My son may have some misguided ideas, but he would never betray his country. And as for Amahle, she was nothing more than a servant. We knew nothing of her... extracurricular activities."

The younger officer scribbled notes as the questioning continued. With each passing minute, the Hartleys felt their carefully constructed world crumbling around them.

As the officers finally left, promising to return with more questions, Richard and Eleanor sat in stunned silence. The weight of their son's choices and their own complicity in an unjust system pressed down upon them.

"What do we do now?" Eleanor whispered, tears streaming down her face.

Richard stared out the window, watching as their neighbors hurried past, avoiding eye contact with the police car in their driveway. He knew their social standing, their entire way of life, was balanced on a knife's edge.

"We weather the storm," he said finally, his voice hollow. "And we pray that James comes to his senses before it's too late."

As the sun climbed higher in the sky, casting harsh light on the opulent furnishings of their home, the Hartleys faced the dawning realization that their world would never be the same again.

THE DIM STREETLIGHTS cast long shadows as James and Amahle made their way through the quiet streets of Port Elizabeth. Their footsteps echoed softly in the night air, their hearts pounding with a mixture of excitement and fear.

"Are you sure about this?" James whispered, glancing nervously over his shoulder.

Amahle nodded, her face set with determination. "We need those documents, James. It's our best chance at exposing the government's corruption."

They approached the nondescript government building, its windows dark and uninviting. James pulled out a set of lock picks, his hands trembling slightly as he worked on the side entrance.

"Where did you learn to do that?" Amahle asked, impressed despite the tension of the moment.

James grinned wryly. "You'd be surprised what they teach you at Oxford."

The lock clicked open, and they slipped inside, the darkness enveloping them. They moved silently through the corridors, guided by the blueprints they had memorized.

As they reached the records room, Amahle stood watch while James began rifling through files. The silence was oppressive, broken only by the rustling of papers.

"I think I've found something," James whispered excitedly, holding up a folder.

Amahle moved closer to examine the documents, their bodies brushing in the cramped space. For a moment, their eyes met, the air between them charged with unspoken emotions.

Suddenly, a beam of light swept across the room. "Hey! Who's there?" a gruff voice called out.

Panic surged through them. James quickly stuffed the documents into his jacket as Amahle grabbed his hand. They ran, hearts pounding, the sound of pursuit close behind.

Bursting out into the night air, they sprinted through alleyways and side streets, not daring to look back. Finally, breathless and shaking, they ducked into a hidden alcove.

As they stood pressed together in the narrow space, adrenaline coursing through their veins, James and Amahle found themselves face to face. The tension between them, built up over weeks of working closely together, finally broke.

Their lips met in a desperate, passionate kiss. For a moment, the danger, the mission, everything else faded away. When they finally pulled apart, both were breathless for reasons beyond their daring escape.

"We should... we should get these documents back to Sipho," Amahle said softly, her voice unsteady.

James nodded, still dazed. "Right. Yes. The mission."

As they made their way back to the safehouse, both were acutely aware that something had fundamentally changed between them. The documents they had risked everything to obtain weighed heavily in James's pocket, but the memory of that kiss, and the complications it brought to their already dangerous situation, weighed even more heavily on their minds.

THE OFFICE OF THE TRUTH Seeker hummed with nervous energy as James hunched over his desk, fingers flying across the typewriter keys. The rhythmic clacking filled the room, punctuated by occasional murmurs from the small group gathered around him.

Marcus, the gruff editor, peered over James's shoulder. "This is dynamite, kid. Are you sure about every detail?"

James nodded without looking up. "I've triple-checked everything. The documents we obtained are irrefutable proof of the government's involvement in the township raids."

As James finished the last paragraph, he pulled the paper from the typewriter with a flourish. The room fell silent as Marcus began to read, his brow furrowing deeper with each line.

"This will blow the lid off everything," Nomsa whispered, her eyes wide. "The international community won't be able to ignore this."

Marcus set the article down, his face grave. "It's good work, James. But publishing this... it's going to bring hell down on all of us. Are we ready for that?"

The team exchanged glances, the weight of the decision hanging heavy in the air. James stood, his voice steady despite his racing heart. "If we don't publish, if we stay silent, then what are we fighting for? This is our chance to make a real difference."

A tense debate erupted, voices rising as they weighed the risks against the potential impact. The exposure could galvanize the anti-apartheid movement, but it could also lead to arrests, or worse.

Finally, Marcus held up his hand, silencing the room. "We've always known this day might come. We got into this business to tell the truth, no matter the cost." He turned to James. "Get it ready for the morning edition. And may God help us all."

As the team sprang into action, preparing the presses and planning distribution, James felt a mix of exhilaration and terror. He thought of Amahle, of the risks she had taken to obtain this information. He thought of his parents, and how this article would affect them.

But as the first copies of the newspaper rolled off the press, headline blazing "GOVERNMENT CORRUPTION EXPOSED: EXCLUSIVE EVIDENCE OF ILLEGAL TOWNSHIP RAIDS," James knew there was no turning back. They had lit the fuse, and now they would face whatever explosion followed.

The Truth Seeker office buzzed with anticipation and fear as dawn approached. They had done their job - told the truth.

Now, they could only wait to see how the world would respond.

THE EARLY MORNING CALM of Port Elizabeth was shattered by the wail of sirens and the thunderous roar of military vehicles. James peered out the window of the safehouse, his heart pounding as he watched armed police units swarming the streets below.

"They're here," he called out, his voice tight with fear.

Sipho burst into the room, his face grim. "We need to evacuate. Now!"

The safehouse erupted into chaos as resistance members scrambled to gather crucial documents and destroy any incriminating evidence. Amahle appeared at James's side, her eyes wide with panic.

"We need to split up," she said urgently. "It's safer that way."

Before James could respond, the sound of splintering wood echoed through the building. "Police! Don't move!"

Sipho ushered them towards a hidden exit. "Go! We'll regroup at the backup location."

James and Amahle sprinted down the back stairs, the shouts of police officers growing louder behind them. As they emerged into the alley, they were met with a scene of utter chaos. Tear gas clouded the air, and the streets were filled with running figures and the sounds of struggle.

"This way!" Amahle yelled, pulling James towards a narrow side street.

They ran, hearts pounding, dodging police cordons and panicked civilians. James could hear Amahle's labored breathing beside him, feel the warmth of her hand in his. Suddenly, a police van screeched to a halt in front of them, cutting off their escape.

"Amahle, run!" James shouted, pushing her towards a small gap between buildings.

As Amahle disappeared from view, James felt rough hands grabbing him, forcing him to the ground. The cold steel of handcuffs bit into his wrists as he was hauled to his feet.

Through the haze of tear gas and confusion, James caught a final glimpse of Amahle's face, horror-stricken as she watched him being dragged away. Then she was gone, swallowed up by the chaos of the crackdown.

As James was shoved into the back of the police van, the reality of their situation crashed over him. The storm they had unleashed with their exposé had broken, and now they were caught in its violent wake, separated and facing an uncertain future.

THE ABANDONED WAREHOUSE echoed with hushed voices and nervous shuffling as the remaining resistance members gathered in the dim light. Amahle stood near the makeshift entrance, her eyes constantly darting to the door, hoping against hope to see James walk through it.

Sipho's deep voice cut through the tension. "We've lost many good people today. But we're not defeated."

A murmur rippled through the group. Nomsa, her arm in a makeshift sling, spoke up. "What do we do now? The government knows our faces, our hideouts."

Sipho's face was grim as he surveyed the battered group. "We have two choices. We can go underground, deeper than ever before. Or..."

"Or what?" Themba asked, his voice tight with fear and anger.

"Or we leave. Cross the border. Continue the fight from exile," Sipho finished.

The warehouse erupted into heated debate. Some argued for staying and fighting, others for the relative safety of neighboring countries. Amahle stood silent, her mind racing.

Finally, she stepped forward, her voice steady despite her inner turmoil. "We can't leave. Not yet. James is still out there, and who knows how many others. We have a responsibility to them, to everyone who's sacrificed for this cause."

Sipho nodded slowly. "Amahle's right. But staying means even greater risks. We'll need to be smarter, more careful than ever before."

As the group began to plan their next moves, Amahle felt the weight of their choices pressing down on her. The path ahead was fraught with danger, but the alternative – abandoning James and their cause – was unthinkable.

In the dim light of the warehouse, surrounded by the remnants of their movement, Amahle made her decision. Whatever came next, whatever sacrifices lay ahead, she would see this fight through to the end. For James, for justice, for the future they had dared to dream of together.

Chapter 6: Trials and Tribulations

The harsh fluorescent light buzzed incessantly, casting stark shadows across the cramped interrogation room. James sat rigidly in an uncomfortable metal chair, his wrists chafing against the handcuffs that bound him to the table. Across from him, Detective Pretorius leaned back in his chair, a predatory gleam in his eyes.

"Let's try this again, Mr. Hartley," Pretorius said, his voice deceptively calm. "Who are your contacts in the resistance?"

James met the detective's gaze steadily, despite the exhaustion that threatened to overwhelm him. "I've told you, I don't know any names."

Pretorius's fist crashed down on the table, causing James to flinch involuntarily. "Don't lie to me, boy! We know you've been working with them. Your little newspaper stunt made that quite clear."

As the detective's voice rose, James's mind drifted, memories flooding back...

The safehouse, weeks earlier. Amahle's hand in his as they pored over documents, her eyes alight with determination. "This is it, James. This could change everything."

James blinked, forcing himself back to the present. "I was just reporting the truth. Isn't that what journalists are supposed to do?"

Pretorius's laugh was cold and mirthless. "Journalist? You're nothing but a traitor. To your country, to your race, to your family."

The words stung, but James held firm. "The only thing I've betrayed is an unjust system."

The detective leaned in close, his breath hot on James's face. "Listen carefully, Hartley. We can make things very difficult for you. For your family. For that pretty little maid you've been so fond of."

James's heart raced at the mention of Amahle, but he kept his expression neutral. "I don't know what you're talking about."

The night of the protest, tear gas burning his eyes. Amahle's face, half-hidden by a scarf, as she helped an elderly woman to safety. The moment their eyes met, a silent understanding passing between them.

Pretorius slammed a file down on the table, spreading photographs across the surface. James recognized faces from the resistance meetings, including his own, caught in grainy black and white.

"We know more than you think," the detective growled. "Give us names, locations, and maybe we can work out a deal. Otherwise..." He left the threat hanging in the air.

James stared at the photos, his resolve wavering for a moment. Then he thought of Amahle, of Sipho, of all those fighting for a better future. He looked up at Pretorius, his voice steady.

"I have nothing more to say."

The detective's face contorted with rage. He stood abruptly, knocking his chair over. "You'll rot in jail, Hartley. You and all your terrorist friends."

As Pretorius stormed out, slamming the door behind him, James slumped in his chair. The interrogation had lasted hours, and he knew it was far from over. But as he sat there, alone in the harsh light, he clung to the memory of Amahle's smile, of the cause they believed in.

Whatever came next, he would not break. He owed them that much.

THE AIR IN THE CRAMPED basement was thick with tension and the acrid smell of cigarette smoke. Amahle stood at the center of the room, her eyes scanning the faces of the dozen or so resistance members who had managed to evade capture. The space, barely lit by a few flickering candles, felt suffocating, but it was the safest place they had left.

"We need to move quickly," Amahle said, her voice low but firm. "Every moment James and the others spend in custody puts them at greater risk."

Sipho, his face haggard from days of evading the police, nodded gravely. "Agreed. But we're severely compromised. Our usual channels, our safe houses – they're all exposed."

A murmur of unease rippled through the group. Nomsa, her arm still in a sling, spoke up. "Maybe... maybe it's time to consider leaving. Crossing the border, regrouping in Botswana or Zambia."

The suggestion hung heavy in the air. Amahle felt a surge of frustration. "And abandon everyone who's been captured? Abandon our cause?"

"It's not abandonment, it's strategy," Themba countered. "We can't help anyone if we're all in jail – or worse."

The room erupted into heated debate. Voices rose, arguments flying back and forth about the best course of action. Amahle watched, a strange calm settling over her despite the chaos.

"Enough!" she shouted suddenly, silencing the room. All eyes turned to her, surprise evident on their faces. Amahle had always been quiet, dependable, but never one to take charge. Until now.

"We're not leaving," she said, her voice steady. "Not while our people are suffering, not while James and the others are imprisoned. We need to be smarter, more careful than ever before. But we will not abandon this fight."

Sipho studied her for a long moment, then nodded slowly. "Amahle's right. We've come too far to give up now. But we need a plan."

As the group began to brainstorm, Amahle felt a mix of determination and fear coursing through her. She thought of James, alone in a cell somewhere, possibly facing torture. She thought of her family in the township, of all those counting on the resistance to bring change.

The path ahead was fraught with danger, but as Amahle looked around at the determined faces of her comrades, she knew they had no choice but to press on. The underground movement would continue, adapting and evolving in the face of adversity.

As the night wore on and plans began to take shape, Amahle silently vowed to do whatever it took to free James and keep the flame of resistance alive. The government may have driven them further underground, but they had not extinguished their spirit. Not yet.

THE HARTLEY ESTATE, once a bastion of privilege and comfort, now felt like a gilded cage. Richard Hartley paced the length of his study, pausing occasionally to glance out the window at the manicured gardens below. The sound of breaking china echoed from somewhere in the house, followed by Eleanor's muffled sobs.

"Damn it all," Richard muttered, running a hand through his graying hair.

A soft knock at the door interrupted his brooding. "Come in," he called out gruffly.

Eleanor entered, her usually impeccable appearance disheveled, eyes red-rimmed from crying. "Richard, we have to do something. We can't just leave James in that... that place."

Richard's jaw clenched. "What would you have me do, Eleanor? Our son has chosen his path. He's thrown everything we've given him back in our faces."

"He's still our son!" Eleanor's voice rose, a hint of hysteria creeping in. "We can't abandon him. Maybe if we speak to the judge, call in some favors—"

"And risk what little standing we have left?" Richard interrupted. "Half our so-called friends won't even return our calls. The club is talking about revoking my membership. Do you know what that would mean for my business?"

Eleanor stared at her husband, a mix of disbelief and disgust crossing her face. "Is that all you care about? Your precious reputation? While our son rots in jail?"

Richard slammed his fist on the desk. "Of course I care! But James made his choice. He chose those... those terrorists over his family, over everything we stand for."

A heavy silence fell between them. Eleanor sank into a chair, suddenly looking older and more fragile than Richard had ever seen her.

"What if..." she began hesitantly, "what if James is right? What if the system we've benefited from all these years is truly unjust?"

Richard froze, staring at his wife in shock. "Eleanor, you can't be serious. This is the way things have always been. It's... it's natural order."

Eleanor met his gaze, a newfound resolve in her eyes. "Is it? Or is that just what we've told ourselves to justify our privilege?"

The question hung in the air, unanswered and heavy with implications. Richard turned away, unable to face the doubt he saw reflected in his wife's eyes.

"I'm going to the police station," Eleanor said, rising from her chair. "I'm going to see our son, with or without you."

As she reached for the door, Richard spoke, his voice barely above a whisper. "Eleanor, if you do this... if you publicly support James... there's no going back. We'll lose everything."

Eleanor paused, her hand on the doorknob. Without turning, she replied, "Maybe it's time we redefine what 'everything' means, Richard."

With that, she left, the soft click of the door closing behind her feeling like the final nail in the coffin of their old life. Richard stood alone in his study, the weight of choice pressing down upon him. Support his son and risk everything, or cling to the remnants of his privileged existence?

As the sun began to set over the Hartley estate, casting long shadows across the room, Richard Hartley faced the most difficult decision of his life. The world was changing around him, and he could no longer ignore the part he had played in perpetuating an unjust system. The question now was whether he had the courage to change with it.

THE PORT ELIZABETH courthouse buzzed with tension as James Hartley and his fellow resistance members were led into the packed courtroom. The air was thick with anticipation, the gallery filled with a mix of anxious family members, stern-faced government officials, and watchful international reporters.

As James took his seat at the defendant's table, his eyes scanned the room, landing briefly on his mother's tear-stained face in the front row. The absence of his father was a painful reminder of the rift his actions had caused.

The judge, a severe-looking man with graying hair, called the court to order. "The State vs. James Hartley and co-defendants, on charges of sedition and terrorism. How do the defendants plead?"

James stood, his voice steady despite the gravity of the moment. "Not guilty, Your Honor."

A murmur rippled through the courtroom as the prosecution began their opening statement, painting James and his comrades as dangerous radicals bent on destabilizing the country.

As the trial progressed, witness after witness was called. Government officials testified about the threat posed by the resistance, while James watched his friends and fellow activists bravely stand their ground under cross-examination.

The turning point came when Amahle was called to the stand. James's heart raced as she walked to the witness box, her head held high despite the palpable hostility in the room.

"Ms. Ndlovu," the prosecutor began, his tone dripping with condescension, "can you explain your relationship with the defendant, James Hartley?"

Amahle's eyes met James's briefly before she answered. "James is my friend and fellow activist. We share a belief in justice and equality for all South Africans."

The prosecutor pounced. "And isn't it true that you used your position as a maid in the Hartley household to gather sensitive information?"

A hush fell over the courtroom. Amahle took a deep breath before responding, her voice clear and unwavering. "I used my position to expose the truth about a system that oppresses millions of people. If that's a crime, then yes, I'm guilty."

Her words seemed to electrify the room. Even some of the white spectators shifted uncomfortably in their seats, unable to ignore the power of her testimony.

As the day wore on, international reporters scribbled furiously in their notebooks. The trial was becoming more than just a local matter; it was shining a spotlight on the injustices of apartheid for the world to see.

When James finally took the stand, he felt the weight of the moment pressing down on him. This was his chance to speak not just to the court, but to the country and the world.

"I stand before you accused of crimes against the state," he began, his voice growing stronger with each word. "But I ask you, what is the greater crime? To speak out against injustice, or to remain silent in the face of oppression?"

As James continued his impassioned testimony, he could see the impact of his words. Some jurors leaned forward, genuinely listening perhaps for the first time. His mother wept openly, a mix of pride and fear on her face.

When the day's proceedings finally came to a close, the outcome of the trial was far from certain. But one thing was clear: the courtroom drama had become a pivotal moment in the fight against apartheid, and its repercussions would be felt far beyond the walls of the Port Elizabeth courthouse.

THE MOON HUNG LOW IN the sky, casting long shadows across the streets of Port Elizabeth. Amahle crouched in the darkness of an alley, her heart pounding as she watched the police van approach. Beside her, Sipho and Nomsa tensed, ready for action.

"Remember," Amahle whispered, "we have one shot at this. If we fail..."

Sipho nodded grimly. "We won't fail. For James and the others, we can't."

As the van slowed at the intersection, Nomsa darted out, throwing a homemade smoke bomb. In the ensuing chaos, Amahle and Sipho rushed the vehicle. The sound of breaking glass and shouts filled the air as they fought to free the prisoners inside.

"James!" Amahle called out, her voice barely audible above the commotion.

A hand grasped hers in the smoke-filled interior. "Amahle? Is that you?"

With a surge of adrenaline, Amahle pulled James from the van. Other resistance members emerged, coughing and disoriented. Sipho's voice cut through the haze: "Move! Now!"

The group sprinted through a maze of back alleys, the sound of police sirens growing closer. Amahle's lungs burned, but she refused to slow down, her hand still clasped tightly in James's.

As they neared the safehouse, a police blockade loomed ahead. Amahle's mind raced, searching for an escape route. Suddenly, a car screeched to a halt beside them. The window rolled down, revealing a face Amahle never expected to see.

"Get in!" Richard Hartley shouted, his eyes wide with fear and determination.

For a moment, everyone froze in disbelief. Then, spurred by the approaching sirens, they piled into the car. As Richard sped away, weaving through side streets, Amahle caught James's eye in the rearview mirror. In that moment, despite the danger still surrounding them, a spark of hope ignited.

The rescue had succeeded, but at what cost? As the city faded behind them, Amahle knew that nothing would ever be the same again. The fight was far from over, but they had struck a blow for freedom that would resonate far beyond this night.

THE SAFE HOUSE WAS a flurry of activity as the newly freed resistance members tended to their wounds and debriefed with their rescuers. In a small, dimly lit room at the back of the building, James and Amahle finally found a moment alone.

They stood facing each other, the air thick with unspoken emotions. James reached out, gently touching Amahle's cheek, his eyes searching hers.

"I can't believe you came for me," he said softly.

Amahle leaned into his touch, her voice barely above a whisper. "I couldn't leave you there. We couldn't."

The sound of approaching footsteps broke the moment. Sipho entered, his face grave. "We need to make a decision, and quickly. The police will be searching everywhere for us."

James and Amahle turned to face him, their hands finding each other instinctively.

Sipho continued, "We have two options. We can try to cross the border into Botswana tonight. It's risky, but we have contacts who can help us continue the fight from exile."

He paused, letting the weight of the alternative hang in the air before speaking again. "Or we stay and go deeper underground. It means even greater danger, but we'd be here, on the front lines."

James and Amahle exchanged a look, months of shared struggle and unspoken feelings passing between them in an instant.

"Whatever we decide," James said, squeezing Amahle's hand, "we decide together."

Amahle nodded, her voice steady as she replied, "We've come too far to turn back now. Our place is here, with our people."

Sipho studied them for a moment, then nodded solemnly. "I had a feeling you'd say that. I'll let the others know."

As he left, James turned to Amahle, pulling her close. "Are you sure about this? It won't be easy."

Amahle met his gaze, her eyes shining with determination and something deeper. "Nothing worth fighting for ever is. But with you by my side, I'm ready for whatever comes next."

Their lips met in a kiss that spoke of shared purpose, of love forged in the fires of struggle. As they broke apart, the sounds of the safe house faded away, leaving them in a bubble of quiet certainty.

Whatever trials lay ahead, whatever sacrifices they would have to make, James and Amahle knew they had made the right choice. Their fight for justice and equality would continue, their love a beacon of hope in the darkness of apartheid South Africa.

The moment of truth had come, and they had chosen their path together.

Chapter 7: The Long Road

The air in the cramped basement was thick with tension and the musty smell of damp earth. James squinted in the dim light cast by a single bare bulb, watching as Amahle pored over a worn map spread across a rickety table. The new hideout, deeper underground than they'd ever ventured before, felt more like a tomb than a refuge.

"Any word from Sipho?" James asked, his voice barely above a whisper.

Amahle shook her head, her brow furrowed with concern. "Nothing since yesterday. The new communication protocols are slowing everything down."

A sudden scrabbling sound from above made them both freeze. James instinctively reached for Amahle's hand, their fingers intertwining in a gesture that had become as natural as breathing. After a tense moment, the noise subsided – just a rat, or perhaps a stray cat prowling the abandoned building above them.

"We can't go on like this forever," James murmured, running his free hand through his unkempt hair. The past weeks of deep hiding had taken their toll, leaving them all ragged and on edge.

Amahle turned to face him, her eyes bright with a fierce determination that never failed to inspire him. "We don't have to. We just need to hold out long enough to rebuild our network. Once we have new safe houses established—"

"If we can find people willing to risk it," James interjected. The recent crackdowns had made even their most stalwart supporters wary.

"We will," Amahle insisted. "The cause is bigger than our fear. People will remember that."

Before James could respond, the secret knock they'd been waiting for sounded at the hidden entrance. Moments later, Nomsa descended the narrow stairs, her face gaunt but her eyes alert.

"I've made contact with a new group in the Eastern Township," she reported without preamble. "They're small, but eager to help. And I've got news from the coast – a shipment might be coming in next week."

James and Amahle exchanged glances. Supplies – food, medicine, and perhaps even weapons – were desperately needed. But every new contact, every operation, brought fresh dangers.

"We'll need to vet them carefully," James said. "We can't afford another close call like last month."

Amahle nodded grimly, remembering the raid that had nearly cost them everything. "I'll reach out to our people in the township, see what they can tell us about this new group."

As they huddled around the map, plotting secure routes and drop points, James felt the familiar mix of hope and dread that had become his constant companion. They were building something here, in the darkness beneath the streets of Port

Elizabeth. A network of resistance that grew stronger with each passing day, despite the government's best efforts to stamp it out.

But the cost was high. James thought of his parents, of the comfortable life he'd left behind. He thought of Amahle's family in the township, at risk every day simply for existing. And he thought of their fallen comrades, whose names they whispered like prayers in the night.

As if sensing his thoughts, Amahle's hand found his again. "We knew it wouldn't be easy," she said softly. "But we're making a difference. Can't you feel it?"

James squeezed her hand, drawing strength from her unwavering conviction. "I can," he replied. And in that moment, in the depths of their underground sanctuary, he allowed himself to believe that their sacrifice would not be in vain. That one day, they would emerge into a South Africa transformed by the seeds of change they were planting in the dark.

THE ONCE-GRAND STUDY of the Hartley estate now felt like a mausoleum, filled with the ghosts of shattered expectations and lost privilege. Richard Hartley sat behind his mahogany desk, staring blankly at the pile of letters before him. Each bore the same message in different words: severed business ties, revoked club memberships, polite but firm social distancing from former friends and associates.

The door creaked open, and Eleanor entered, her face drawn and tired. "The gardener's just given his notice," she said softly. "That's the last of the staff gone."

Richard nodded numbly. The consequences of his decision to help James escape had been swift and merciless. Their carefully constructed world was crumbling around them, and he found himself struggling to care.

"Perhaps it's for the best," he murmured, more to himself than to Eleanor. "We can't afford to keep them on anyway, not with the business in shambles."

Eleanor moved to stand beside him, her hand resting lightly on his shoulder. "Richard," she began hesitantly, "I've been thinking. Maybe... maybe it's time we considered leaving."

He looked up at her, surprise momentarily breaking through his melancholy. "Leaving? And go where?"

"Anywhere," Eleanor replied, a hint of her old fire returning to her eyes. "Somewhere we can start fresh, without the weight of all this..." she gestured vaguely at the trappings of their former life.

Richard stood, moving to the window. The manicured gardens, once a source of pride, now seemed to mock him with their perfection. "And what would we do, Eleanor? Who would we be, if not the Hartleys of Port Elizabeth?"

Eleanor joined him at the window, her voice soft but firm. "We'd be James's parents. We'd be people who finally chose to stand on the right side of history, no matter the cost."

Richard turned to face his wife, really seeing her for the first time in weeks. The woman before him was not the society matron he'd married, concerned with appearances and status. This Eleanor was stronger, more resilient – changed, as he was, by the choices their son had forced them to confront.

"It won't be easy," he said, voicing the fear that had been gnawing at him. "We're not young anymore, Eleanor. To start over..."

She took his hand, squeezing it gently. "Nothing worth doing ever is. But Richard, I can't bear to stay here, pretending that the world isn't changing around us. James showed us the truth, and now we have a choice to make."

As the sun began to set, casting long shadows across the study, Richard Hartley felt something shift within him. The anger and resentment he'd been nursing since James's departure began to give way to a tentative hope.

"Where would we even begin?" he asked, his voice barely above a whisper.

Eleanor's smile was small but genuine. "We start by contacting James. By offering whatever support we can to him and his cause. And then... then we figure out the rest together."

Richard nodded slowly, the weight of decision settling over him. They would face challenges, he knew. Rebuilding their lives would be a monumental task. But as he looked at Eleanor, at the determination shining in her eyes, he felt a spark of the same courage that had driven their son to fight for what was right.

"Together, then," he said, sealing their new path with a gentle kiss.

As night fell over the Hartley estate, Richard and Eleanor began the painstaking process of dismantling their old life. With each possession sorted, each memory confronted, they moved closer to a future neither had imagined – but one they now embraced with cautious hope.

THE BUSTLING NEWSROOM of The New York Times hummed with activity as reporters and editors rushed to meet their deadlines. Among them, Sarah Thompson, a seasoned foreign correspondent, hunched over her desk, her fingers flying across the keyboard as she crafted her latest piece on the unfolding situation in South Africa.

"Thompson!" her editor called out. "What's the latest on that trial in Port Elizabeth?"

Sarah looked up, her eyes bright with excitement. "It's big, Jack. Really big. The escape of James Hartley and the other activists has blown this wide open. I've got sources saying it's causing major diplomatic headaches for the South African government."

As if on cue, the teletype machine in the corner began to clatter. A young intern rushed over, tearing off the paper and running it to Jack's desk. The editor's eyebrows shot up as he read.

"Listen up, everyone!" he shouted, silencing the room. "The United Nations Security Council has just passed a resolution condemning the South African government's actions. They're calling for immediate sanctions."

A ripple of excitement passed through the newsroom. Sarah felt a surge of adrenaline; this was the kind of story that could change the course of history.

Across the Atlantic, in the halls of the British Parliament, a heated debate was underway. Sir Reginald Fawcett, a conservative MP, pounded his fist on the podium.

"We cannot stand idly by while a member of the Commonwealth flouts basic human rights!" he declared, his voice echoing through the chamber. "The time has come for Britain to take a stand against apartheid!"

In Stockholm, the Nobel Committee convened an emergency meeting. The chairman, Erik Lundberg, addressed his colleagues with grave seriousness.

"The events in South Africa have captured the world's attention," he began. "I propose we consider the resistance movement, and specifically individuals like James Hartley and Amahle Ndlovu, for this year's Peace Prize. Their courage in the face of oppression embodies the very spirit of Alfred Nobel's vision."

Meanwhile, in a small office in Lusaka, Zambia, Oliver Tambo, the exiled leader of the African National Congress, pored over reports from South Africa. A smile played at the corners of his mouth as he read about the daring escape and the international reaction it had sparked.

"At last," he murmured to himself. "The world is waking up to our struggle."

Back in Port Elizabeth, deep in their underground hideout, James and Amahle huddled around a crackling shortwave radio. The BBC World Service announcer's voice cut through the static:

"In an unprecedented move, the United States Congress has passed a comprehensive anti-apartheid act, imposing strict economic sanctions on South Africa. The bill, which passed with a veto-proof majority, represents a significant shift in U.S. foreign policy..."

James and Amahle exchanged a look of cautious hope. Their fight was far from over, but for the first time, they felt the full weight of international support behind them.

"It's working," Amahle whispered, her eyes shining with unshed tears. "All our sacrifices, all the risks we've taken... it's finally making a difference."

James squeezed her hand, his voice thick with emotion. "This is just the beginning. The world is watching now. We can't let them down."

As the radio continued to relay news of global reactions and increasing pressure on the South African government, James and Amahle allowed themselves a moment of quiet celebration. The road ahead was still long and fraught with danger, but the international spotlight now shining on their cause gave them renewed strength for the battles to come.

THE NARROW ALLEYWAYS of Port Elizabeth's township were shrouded in pre-dawn darkness as James and Amahle moved silently through the shadows. Their mission was simple but dangerous: deliver vital medical supplies to a safe house that had been cut off from their usual supply routes.

James's heart pounded as they approached the final stretch, a poorly lit street that offered little cover. He glanced at Amahle, her face a mask of concentration in the dim light. They had done this a dozen times before, but each operation brought new risks.

Suddenly, the beam of a flashlight cut through the darkness. "Hey! You there! Stop!" a gruff voice called out.

James and Amahle froze for a split second before instinct took over. Without a word, they bolted, James clutching the precious bag of supplies to his chest as they ran.

The sound of heavy footsteps and shouted orders echoed behind them as they weaved through the maze-like streets. James's lungs burned, but adrenaline pushed him forward. He felt Amahle's hand grab his arm, pulling him sharply to the left into a hidden alcove.

They pressed themselves against the wall, hardly daring to breathe as the patrol thundered past their hiding spot. James could feel Amahle's heart racing where her body was pressed against his.

Long minutes passed before they dared to move. Amahle peered out, her whisper barely audible. "I think we're clear."

As they cautiously emerged, the gravity of their near-capture hit James like a physical blow. He turned to Amahle, his voice shaky. "That was too close. If they had caught us…"

Amahle's eyes met his, a mix of fear and determination evident in her gaze. "But they didn't. We're still here, still fighting."

James nodded, drawing strength from her resolve. They had to keep moving, had to complete their mission. But as they resumed their journey, now hyper-aware of every shadow and sound, James knew they would need to reevaluate their tactics. The risks were growing, and they couldn't afford many more close calls like this.

The safe house was just ahead, a faint light in a window their signal that it was secure to approach. As they slipped inside, delivering their precious cargo, James and Amahle shared a look of silent understanding. Their bond, forged in moments of danger like this, had grown into something unbreakable. Whatever challenges lay ahead, they would face them together.

THE ABANDONED WAREHOUSE echoed with hushed voices as the core members of the resistance gathered. James and Amahle sat side by side, their shoulders touching, a silent reminder of their recent close call. Sipho stood at the head of the makeshift table, his face grave.

"We've received intelligence," Sipho began, his voice low but carrying clearly through the tense silence. "The government is planning to implement a new pass law, even more restrictive than the current one. It would essentially trap people in the townships, make it nearly impossible to work or travel."

A ripple of anger and dismay passed through the group. Nomsa spoke up, her voice tight with fury. "We can't let this happen. We have to do something."

Sipho nodded, unfolding a map on the table. "That's why I've called this meeting. We have an opportunity – perhaps our biggest yet – to strike a significant blow against the apartheid system."

As Sipho outlined the plan – a coordinated series of actions targeting government offices responsible for the new law – James felt a mix of excitement and trepidation. This was bigger than anything they'd attempted before, with potentially far-reaching consequences.

"The risks are enormous," Themba pointed out, voicing the concern evident on many faces. "If we're caught, it won't just be jail. We could be looking at treason charges, maybe even..."

He didn't need to finish the sentence. Execution was a very real possibility.

Amahle leaned forward, her eyes blazing with determination. "But if we succeed, we could derail this law before it's implemented. We could save countless lives, give hope to those who've lost it."

The room erupted into debate, voices rising as they weighed the potential impact against the dangers. James listened intently, his mind racing. Finally, he stood, drawing all eyes to him.

"This is what we've been fighting for," he said, his voice steady. "A chance to make real change, to show the world that apartheid can be challenged. Yes, the risks are high, but so are the stakes if we do nothing."

Amahle stood beside him, taking his hand. "James is right. We didn't go underground, didn't sacrifice everything, just to play it safe. This is our moment."

Sipho looked around the room, gauging the mood. Slowly, heads began to nod in agreement. The decision was made.

"Very well," Sipho said, his voice solemn. "We move forward. James, Amahle – I want you two to take point on coordinating the Port Elizabeth operation. It's crucial we hit all targets simultaneously."

As the group delved into the details of the plan, James and Amahle shared a look of understanding. This mission could change everything – for the country, for the resistance, for them. The road ahead was fraught with danger, but they were ready to walk it together.

The turning point had arrived. There was no going back now.

THE PRE-DAWN DARKNESS cloaked Port Elizabeth in shadows as James and Amahle made their final preparations. Their small flat, serving as a temporary safe house, was a flurry of quiet but intense activity.

"Communications check," James whispered, adjusting his earpiece.

Amahle nodded, her fingers dancing over a makeshift radio set. "All teams reporting in. We're go for phase one."

They shared a look, years of shared struggle and unspoken feelings passing between them in an instant. Amahle reached out, squeezing James's hand. "Be careful out there."

"You too," he replied, his voice thick with emotion. "Remember, if anything goes wrong—"

"Rendezvous at point Charlie," Amahle finished. "I know. But it won't come to that. We've planned for everything."

As they stepped out into the cool night air, the weight of their mission settled over them. This was it – their biggest operation yet, with the potential to deal a crippling blow to the apartheid regime's new pass law plans.

James and Amahle split up, each heading to their designated targets. The streets were eerily quiet, the calm before the storm. As James approached the government records office, he caught sight of Themba's team moving into position across the street.

"Team A in place," he murmured into his comm.

"Copy that," Amahle's voice crackled in his ear. "Team B ready. Awaiting final signal."

James's heart raced as he watched the seconds tick by on his watch. Everything hinged on precise timing and flawless execution.

Suddenly, a burst of static in his earpiece made him wince. "James!" Amahle's urgent whisper came through. "We've got movement at the police station. Unexpected patrol."

James felt a surge of adrenaline. This wasn't part of the plan. "Can you evade?"

"Negative," Amahle replied, her voice tense. "They're heading right for us. We need to abort."

James's mind raced. Aborting now would mean months of planning wasted, possibly their only chance at stopping the new law. But pushing forward could mean capture – or worse.

"Hold position," he decided, his voice steady despite the fear coursing through him. "I'm on my way. We're not giving up yet."

As James melted back into the shadows, moving swiftly towards Amahle's location, the fate of their mission – and possibly the entire resistance – hung in the balance. The night was far from over, and the real challenges were only just beginning.

Chapter 8: The Reckoning

The night air was thick with tension as James raced through the shadowy streets of Port Elizabeth, his heart pounding in rhythm with his footsteps. Amahle's urgent message still echoed in his ears: "Unexpected patrol. Need to abort." But James wasn't ready to give up – not when they were so close to dealing a crippling blow to the apartheid regime's plans.

As he neared Amahle's position, James slowed his pace, every sense on high alert. The distant wail of police sirens sent a chill down his spine. He pressed himself against a crumbling brick wall, peering around the corner.

There, barely visible in the dim streetlight, he saw Amahle and her team huddled behind a rusted dumpster. A police van crawled down the street, its searchlight sweeping back and forth across the buildings.

James's mind raced. They needed a distraction, something to draw the police away without raising suspicion. His eyes landed on a pile of discarded bottles near his feet. It was risky, but they were out of options.

With a silent prayer, James grabbed a bottle and hurled it down a side alley, away from Amahle's position. The crash of shattering glass shattered the night's silence.

The effect was immediate. The police van's engine revved, and it sped towards the source of the noise. James used the moment of confusion to sprint across the street, sliding into cover beside Amahle.

"James!" she whispered, relief and worry mingling in her voice. "What are you doing here?"

"Changing the plan," he replied, his eyes scanning their surroundings. "We can still do this, but we need to move now."

Amahle nodded, years of trust and shared struggle evident in her unwavering gaze. "What's the play?"

James quickly outlined a modified version of their original plan, adapting to the increased police presence. It was dangerous, with even smaller margins for error than before, but it was their only shot.

As they prepared to move out, the sound of approaching footsteps froze them in place. A beam of light cut through the darkness, inching closer to their hiding spot. James and Amahle held their breath, bodies tense and ready to run.

The light paused, mere inches from revealing their position. Long seconds ticked by, each moment an eternity. Then, mercifully, the beam swung away, accompanied by the crackle of a radio: "All clear in sector four. Moving to the next grid."

As the footsteps faded, James and Amahle shared a look of grim determination. They had evaded capture by the slimmest of margins, but the night was far from over. With a nod to the rest of the team, they slipped out of their hiding place and melted into the shadows.

The mission was still on, but now the stakes were higher than ever. One wrong move, one moment of bad luck, and everything they had fought for could come crashing down. As they moved through the darkened streets, James felt the weight of their cause pressing down on him. They were in the crosshairs now, and there was no turning back.

THE SAFE HOUSE WAS thick with tension as James and Amahle entered, their faces grim. The rest of the resistance members looked up expectantly, hope quickly fading as they read the situation in the newcomers' expressions.

Sipho stepped forward, his voice low and controlled. "What happened?"

James ran a hand through his hair, exhaustion evident in every movement. "We had to abort. Police presence was heavier than expected. We managed to complete part of the operation, but..."

"But what?" Themba interrupted, his voice sharp with accusation. "We've been planning this for months! How could you just give up?"

Amahle's eyes flashed. "We didn't give up. We made a tactical decision to ensure the safety of our people and preserve our network. Would you rather we'd all been captured?"

The room erupted into heated arguments. Accusations flew back and forth, months of pent-up stress and fear bubbling to the surface. James watched as the unity they had worked so hard to build began to fracture before his eyes.

"Enough!" Sipho's voice cut through the chaos. "This infighting solves nothing. We need to assess the damage and plan our next move."

As the group settled into a tense debriefing, James caught Amahle's eye. They shared a look of understanding – the real battle now would be holding the resistance together in the face of this setback.

Nomsa spoke up, her voice trembling slightly. "How did they know? The police shouldn't have been there. Someone must have tipped them off."

A heavy silence fell over the room as the implication sank in. The possibility of a traitor in their midst had always been a fear, but now it loomed large and undeniable.

James stepped into the center of the room, his voice steady despite the turmoil he felt. "We can't let suspicion tear us apart. That's exactly what the regime wants. We've come too far, sacrificed too much, to fall apart now."

Amahle moved to stand beside him, her presence a source of strength. "James is right. We need to focus on what we did accomplish tonight and how we can build on it. The fight isn't over – it's only beginning."

As the night wore on, the group slowly began to regroup, analyzing their partial success and planning their next steps. The tension in the room remained, but a fragile sense of purpose was restored.

James and Amahle found a quiet moment alone as the others dispersed to their tasks. "We're walking a tightrope," James murmured, the weight of leadership heavy on his shoulders.

Amahle squeezed his hand. "We'll get through this. We have to."

As dawn broke over Port Elizabeth, the resistance regrouped, battered but not broken. The fallout from the night's events had shaken them, but it had also steeled their resolve. The road ahead was more uncertain than ever, but they would face it together.

THE RESISTANCE SAFE house buzzed with nervous energy as James pored over maps and reports spread across a rickety table. Amahle stood nearby, her brow furrowed in concentration as she cross-referenced dates and locations.

"There," James said suddenly, jabbing his finger at a point on the map. "Every time we've had a close call or a compromised operation, it's been within this sector."

Amahle leaned in, her eyes widening. "That's Themba's area of responsibility."

A heavy silence fell between them as the implication sank in. James ran a hand through his hair, his voice barely above a whisper. "We can't jump to conclusions. We need proof."

As if on cue, Sipho entered the room, his face grave. "We've got a problem. Our contact in the police force just sent word. They've been getting regular tips about our movements, and the source..." He paused, his eyes meeting James's. "The source is coming from inside our organization."

The news spread through the safe house like wildfire. Accusations flew, old grudges resurfaced, and the fragile trust that held the resistance together began to fray.

James watched as suspicion turned friend against friend. He caught sight of Themba, standing apart from the others, his face a mask of worry. Was it guilt, or just the natural fear of being wrongly accused?

Amahle's voice cut through the chaos. "We can't tear ourselves apart over this. It's exactly what the regime wants."

James nodded, stepping forward to address the group. "Amahle's right. We need to approach this methodically. From now on, we operate in smaller cells. Information is shared on a need-to-know basis only."

As the resistance members grudgingly agreed to the new protocols, James pulled Sipho aside. "We need to set a trap," he murmured. "Feed different information to different people and see what makes its way to the authorities."

Sipho nodded grimly. "It's risky, but it might be our only option."

Over the next days, tension in the safe house reached a fever pitch. Every glance, every whispered conversation, became suspect. James and Amahle worked tirelessly, coordinating with their police contact and meticulously tracking the flow of information.

The breakthrough came on a rainy Tuesday afternoon. James burst into Amahle's room, his face a mix of triumph and anguish. "We've got him," he said, his voice hoarse. "It's Themba. He's been feeding information to the police for months."

Amahle's hand flew to her mouth, shock and betrayal evident in her eyes. "Are you sure?"

James nodded, producing a stack of documents. "Our contact came through. Bank records, meeting logs, everything. Themba's been playing us from the start."

As the reality of Themba's betrayal sank in, James felt a deep sadness settle over him. The revelation of Themba's betrayal was a bitter victory. They had rooted out the mole, but at the cost of another friend, another comrade lost to the cruel realities of their struggle.

The resistance had survived this test, but James knew the scars of suspicion and betrayal would not fade easily. As they prepared to face Themba, he squeezed Amahle's hand, drawing strength from her presence. Whatever came next, they would face it together, their bond stronger than ever in the face of treachery.

THE MORNING SUN CAST long shadows across the manicured lawn of the Hartley estate as Richard and Eleanor Hartley stood hand in hand on their front porch. A small crowd of reporters and curious onlookers had gathered at the gate, alerted by rumors of an impending announcement.

Richard cleared his throat, his voice wavering slightly as he began to speak. "For too long, we have been silent in the face of injustice. Today, that silence ends."

Eleanor squeezed his hand, offering silent support as he continued.

"Our son, James, chose to stand against the apartheid system, and we... we were wrong to doubt him. Today, we stand with James and all those fighting for equality and justice in South Africa."

A ripple of shock passed through the crowd. Cameras flashed as Richard held up a document.

"This is our resignation from all social clubs and business associations that support or benefit from apartheid. We call on our friends and colleagues to examine their own consciences and do the same."

Eleanor stepped forward, her voice clear and unwavering. "We have also established a fund to support the families of political prisoners and to aid in the legal defense of anti-apartheid activists."

As the Hartleys continued their declaration, the reaction from the crowd was mixed. Some applauded, while others shouted accusations of betrayal. In the back, a group of their former friends turned away in disgust.

Suddenly, a rock sailed through the air, shattering a window behind them. Richard instinctively moved to shield Eleanor, but she stood her ground, chin raised defiantly.

"We understand that our stand may cost us old friendships and social standing," Richard continued, his voice stronger now. "But we can no longer enjoy privilege built on the suffering of others. We choose to stand on the right side of history, whatever the personal cost."

As they finished their statement, chaos erupted. Journalists shouted questions, supporters clashed with angry neighbors, and in the distance, police sirens wailed.

Richard and Eleanor retreated into their home, the door closing on the tumult outside. In the sudden quiet of their foyer, they embraced, both trembling with the magnitude of what they had done.

"Do you think James will hear about this?" Eleanor whispered.

Richard nodded, a mix of pride and worry in his eyes. "I'm sure he will. And I hope... I hope he understands that we finally see the truth he's been fighting for."

As the sounds of the crowd outside grew louder, Richard and Eleanor Hartley stood together, facing an uncertain future but secure in the knowledge that they had finally taken a stand for what was right.

THE UNDERGROUND RESISTANCE hideout thrummed with nervous energy as James and Amahle huddled over a makeshift planning table, surrounded by their most trusted allies. Maps, intelligence reports, and hastily scribbled notes covered every available surface.

"We have less than 48 hours before the government implements the new pass laws," James said, his voice taut with urgency. "If we don't act now, thousands will be trapped in the townships, cut off from work and resources."

Amahle nodded grimly, tracing a route on the central map. "Our inside source confirms that the final authorization documents are being moved to the central administration building tonight. If we can intercept and expose them, it could delay implementation and give us time to rally more international support."

Sipho, his face etched with worry, spoke up. "It's a massive risk. Security will be tighter than ever after our last operation."

"We don't have a choice," James replied, meeting each of their gazes in turn. "This is what we've been fighting for. We can't back down now."

As the group delved into the details of their plan, the stakes became painfully clear. This wasn't just another operation; it was possibly their last chance to make a significant impact before the government's stranglehold tightened further.

The cool night air nipped at James and Amahle's faces as they approached the imposing administration building. Their hearts raced, but years of working together allowed them to maintain an outward calm. They were dressed in nondescript overalls, tool belts slung low on their hips, and each carried a battered toolbox.

"Remember," James murmured as they neared the service entrance, "we're just here to fix the faulty wiring in the basement. Keep your head down and let me do the talking."

Amahle nodded, adjusting her cap lower over her eyes. As they reached the door, a burly security guard stepped out of the shadows, his hand resting casually on his holstered weapon.

"Identification," he grunted, eyeing them suspiciously.

James produced two forged worker passes, his hand steady despite the adrenaline coursing through his veins. "Electrical maintenance," he said, adopting a bored tone. "Got a call about some issues in the lower levels."

The guard scrutinized the passes, then glanced at his clipboard. After what felt like an eternity, he nodded curtly. "Fine. But be quick about it. No wandering."

As the heavy door clanged shut behind them, James and Amahle shared a brief look of relief. They had made it inside, but the real challenge was just beginning. Navigating the labyrinthine corridors of the building's lower levels, they knew that one wrong turn, one misplaced word, could spell disaster for their mission and for the countless lives depending on its success.

James and Amahle crept through the dimly lit corridors, their footsteps echoing softly despite their best efforts. As they rounded a corner, they froze – a guard was standing at the far end of the hallway, his back to them but clearly alert.

"We need to get past him," Amahle whispered, her breath warm against James's ear. "The documents should be just beyond that security door."

James nodded, his mind racing. They couldn't risk a confrontation, but turning back wasn't an option. Suddenly, the guard turned, his eyes widening as he spotted them.

"Hey! You there!" he called out, his hand moving to his radio.

James stepped forward, forcing a smile. "Evening, sir. We're just here to check on that faulty wiring. Been giving everyone headaches, I hear."

The guard's eyes narrowed. "I wasn't informed of any maintenance tonight. Let me see your work order."

As James fumbled in his pockets, buying time, a loud crash echoed from somewhere above them. The guard's head snapped up, momentarily distracted. In that split second, Amahle moved with lightning speed, her hand striking a precise point on the guard's neck. He crumpled to the ground, unconscious but breathing.

"Nice timing," James murmured, knowing their outside team had created the diversion exactly when needed.

Amahle was already dragging the guard into a nearby supply closet. "We have minutes at best before someone notices he's missing. Let's move."

James and Amahle moved swiftly down the corridor, their footsteps echoing softly despite their best efforts to remain silent. They reached the heavy steel door that led to the records room, its imposing presence a stark reminder of the sensitive information it protected.

Amahle pulled out a small electronic device from her toolbox, attaching it to the keypad lock. The device flickered to life, cycling through number combinations at a dizzying speed. Each second felt like an eternity as they waited, hyper-aware of every distant sound in the building.

"Come on, come on," James muttered under his breath, his eyes darting between the device and the empty corridor behind them.

After what seemed like hours but was merely minutes, the device beeped softly, and the lock disengaged with a quiet click. They shared a brief look of relief before slipping into the dimly lit room.

Rows of filing cabinets lined the walls, but their target stood out immediately – a large safe in the corner, its polished surface gleaming dully in the low light. James approached it, running his hands along the edges, searching for any hidden alarm triggers.

Amahle joined him, producing a stethoscope-like device from her bag. She pressed it against the safe's door, listening intently as she slowly turned the dial. The only sounds in the room were their shallow breathing and the faint click of the safe's mechanism.

Suddenly, a noise from the corridor outside made them both freeze. Footsteps, growing louder. James's heart raced as he looked at Amahle, still working on the safe. They were so close, but discovery now would mean failure – and likely imprisonment or worse.

The footsteps paused just outside the door. James held his breath, every muscle in his body tense, ready to spring into action if needed. After a moment that felt like an eternity, the footsteps resumed, fading away down the hall.

Amahle let out a shaky breath, returning her focus to the safe. A few more tense minutes passed before a final, satisfying click signaled success. The safe door swung open, revealing stacks of documents inside.

"This is it," James whispered, quickly but carefully leafing through the papers. "The implementation orders, the new zone restrictions, everything we need to expose their plans."

As they hurriedly photographed the most crucial documents and gathered what physical evidence they could safely take, the weight of their accomplishment began to sink in. They had the proof they needed, but the most dangerous part of their mission still lay ahead – getting out of the building and disseminating the information before it was too late.

With one last sweep to ensure they left no trace of their presence, James and Amahle prepared to make their escape, the stolen documents secured and hidden within their disguises. The night was far from over, but they had cleared a crucial hurdle in their race against time.

As dawn broke over Port Elizabeth, James and Amahle raced through the awakening streets, the stolen documents clutched tightly to their chests. They had succeeded in obtaining the evidence, but now faced the equally daunting task of disseminating it before the authorities could suppress the information.

With government forces closing in and time running out, James and Amahle knew that the next few hours would determine not just the fate of their mission, but the future of countless lives hanging in the balance. The race against time had begun, and failure was not an option.

THE SUN HUNG LOW ON the horizon, casting long shadows across the streets of Port Elizabeth as James and Amahle approached the imposing government building. Their hearts raced, knowing that everything they had fought for came down to this moment.

"Are you ready?" James asked, his voice barely above a whisper.

Amahle nodded, her jaw set with determination. "Let's end this."

They moved swiftly, blending in with the small crowd of late-working bureaucrats leaving for the day. As they neared the entrance, a commotion erupted behind them.

"There they are!" a gruff voice shouted. "Stop them!"

James and Amahle broke into a run, pushing through the revolving doors and into the marble-floored lobby. Security guards scrambled to intercept them, but years of evading capture had honed their reflexes.

"Split up!" Amahle called out, veering left towards the stairwell.

James nodded, sprinting right towards the elevators. He could hear the heavy footfalls of pursuers close behind.

As Amahle bounded up the stairs, her mind raced through their plan. The evidence they had gathered needed to reach the office of the sympathetic official on the fifth floor. If they could get it there, it would be broadcast to the world, exposing the government's brutal new policies before they could be implemented.

James jammed his finger on the elevator button, ducking just as a security guard's baton swung over his head. The doors slid open, and he threw himself inside, frantically pressing the close button.

As the elevator ascended, James caught his breath, knowing Amahle would be making her way up the stairs. They had planned for this, knowing that by splitting up, at least one of them had a chance of succeeding.

On the fifth floor, Amahle burst through the stairwell door, nearly colliding with a startled clerk. She pressed the envelope containing their evidence into the man's hands.

"Get this to Minister Venter's office immediately," she gasped. "It's a matter of national importance."

Before the clerk could respond, two security guards rounded the corner. Amahle took off running again, leading them away from the crucial evidence.

James emerged from the elevator just in time to see Amahle sprinting down the hallway, pursuers close behind. Their eyes met for a brief moment, a lifetime of understanding passing between them.

With a nod, James turned and ran in the opposite direction, shouting to draw attention away from Amahle and the clerk now hurrying towards Minister Venter's office.

As alarms blared and the building went into lockdown, James and Amahle found themselves cornered in opposite wings of the building. They could hear the heavy boots of security forces closing in.

In that moment, as the culmination of their years-long struggle hung in the balance, James and Amahle shared a silent, invisible connection. Whatever happened next, they had given everything for their cause. The truth was out there now, making its way to those who could use it to bring change.

The sound of doors bursting open echoed from both ends of the building. James squared his shoulders, ready to face whatever came next. Across the building, Amahle did the same.

The showdown had begun, and the fate of their mission – and perhaps the entire anti-apartheid movement – hung in the balance.

Chapter 9: Dawn of Change

The air in the government building crackled with tension as alarms blared and shouted orders echoed through the corridors. James pressed himself against the wall of a narrow alcove, his heart pounding as a group of security guards rushed past. Across the building, Amahle crouched behind a large potted plant, her eyes darting between the elevators and the stairwell door.

Suddenly, a voice boomed over the building's intercom system: "Attention all personnel. This is Minister Venter. I have just received information of vital national importance. All security forces are to stand down immediately. I repeat, stand down."

James and Amahle exchanged looks of disbelief from their hiding spots. Had they actually succeeded?

Outside, the streets of Port Elizabeth erupted into chaos. Word spread like wildfire as people gathered around radios and television sets in homes, shops, and bars. The government's plans for even harsher pass laws and racial segregation, exposed in stark detail, shocked even those who thought they'd seen the worst of apartheid.

"Did you hear?" a breathless young man shouted as he ran down the street. "They were going to forcibly relocate entire communities! It's all coming out now!"

In the township, people poured out of their homes, a mix of anger and hope fueling impromptu gatherings. Sipho stood atop an overturned crate, his voice carrying over the crowd: "This is our moment! The world can no longer ignore what's happening here!"

Back in the government building, James and Amahle cautiously emerged from hiding, making their way towards Minister Venter's office. They found the minister surrounded by a flurry of activity, phones ringing off the hook and aides rushing in and out with urgent messages.

Venter looked up as they entered, his face a mix of exhaustion and grim determination. "You two have no idea what you've just unleashed," he said, but there was a hint of respect in his voice.

As night fell over Port Elizabeth, the city simmered with an energy that was part celebration, part apprehension. The full ramifications of the day's events were yet to be felt, but everyone could sense that something fundamental had shifted.

James and Amahle stood on the roof of the resistance's safe house, looking out over the city lights. Amahle's hand found James's, squeezing it tightly.

"What happens now?" she asked softly.

James shook his head, his eyes fixed on the horizon. "I don't know. But whatever comes next, we face it together."

As sirens wailed in the distance and the murmur of crowds drifted up from the streets below, James and Amahle knew that the real battle was just beginning. The aftermath of their actions would reshape not just their lives, but the future of an entire nation.

THE BUSTLING NEWSROOM of the BBC World Service in London fell silent as the latest wire reports from South Africa flashed across the screens. Journalists and editors stared in disbelief at the flood of information pouring in.

"My God," whispered veteran correspondent Emma Bradbury, her eyes wide. "They were planning to implement a system that would make the current pass laws look lenient by comparison."

The editor-in-chief, John Blackwell, emerged from his office, his face grim. "This is it, people. The story we've been waiting for. I want all hands on deck. Emma, you're on air in ten minutes. Give me a global implications angle."

As Emma rushed to prepare her broadcast, phones began ringing off the hook. Diplomats, human rights organizations, and political leaders from around the world were clamoring for information and demanding statements.

In New York, the United Nations Security Council convened an emergency session. The U.S. Ambassador to the UN, voice tight with controlled anger, addressed the assembly:

"The information revealed today in South Africa represents a shocking escalation of the apartheid regime's oppressive policies. The United States calls for immediate sanctions and a full investigation into these planned human rights violations."

Across the globe, from Washington D.C. to Moscow, from Beijing to London, governments scrambled to respond.

Emergency meetings were called, statements drafted, and diplomatic back channels buzzed with activity.

In Oslo, the Nobel Committee huddled in an unscheduled meeting. The chairman spoke in hushed tones: "These revelations change everything. We must consider the implications for this year's Peace Prize."

As day turned to night in Europe, the full weight of the exposed information began to sink in. On television screens worldwide, images of protests erupting across South Africa were juxtaposed with solemn-faced world leaders promising action.

In a small flat in London, an exiled South African activist named Mandla watched the unfolding events with tears in his eyes. He picked up the phone with trembling hands, dialing a number he knew by heart.

"Mama?" he said when the call connected. "It's happening. The world finally sees. Maybe... maybe I can come home soon."

As the global shockwaves continued to reverberate, it became clear that the actions of James, Amahle, and their fellow resistance members had not just exposed government plans – they had fundamentally altered the course of history. The world's eyes were now firmly fixed on South Africa, and the pressure for change was building to an unstoppable crescendo.

THE AIR IN THE CRAMPED basement hideout crackled with energy as resistance members from across Port Elizabeth gathered. The room, usually somber and tense, now buzzed with excitement and renewed determination.

Sipho stood at the center, his voice carrying over the murmurs: "Comrades, the moment we've been fighting for is here. The world now sees the truth we've known all along."

Amahle stepped forward, her eyes bright with purpose. "But we can't rest now. This is when we push harder than ever."

James nodded in agreement. "The government is in chaos, but they'll regroup soon. We need to strike while they're off balance."

The room erupted into a flurry of ideas and plans. Nomsa, her arm still in a sling, spoke up: "We should organize mass protests in every major city. Show them our numbers."

"And reach out to international media," added Zolani, a newer member who had joined after being inspired by recent events. "Keep the world's eyes on us."

As the night wore on, a comprehensive strategy took shape. Teams were assigned to coordinate protests, establish communication networks with other resistance cells across the country, and liaise with sympathetic journalists and diplomats.

Outside, the streets of Port Elizabeth thrummed with an energy not felt in years. People gathered in small groups, discussing the revelations in hushed but urgent tones. In the township, impromptu meetings sprang up, with long-time activists welcoming curious newcomers.

At dawn, as the resistance members emerged from their planning session, they were met with an unprecedented sight. Hundreds of people, of all races, had gathered outside their hideout. A young woman stepped forward, her voice trembling but determined:

"We want to help. Tell us what to do."

James and Amahle exchanged a look of hope and trepidation. The resistance was no longer just their small, dedicated group. It had become a movement, ready to change the course of history.

As the sun rose over Port Elizabeth, casting long shadows across the awakening city, the air was charged with possibility. The resistance was rallying, stronger and more united than ever before, ready to face whatever challenges lay ahead in their fight for justice and equality.

THE OPULENT OFFICE of President P.W. Botha, usually a bastion of order and control, now resembled a war room in disarray. Maps and reports littered every surface, and the air was thick with cigarette smoke and tension.

"How the hell did this happen?" Botha thundered, slamming his fist on the polished mahogany desk. His inner circle of advisors and ministers flinched at the outburst.

Minister of Law and Order, Adriaan Vlok, stepped forward, his face ashen. "Mr. President, we're still piecing together the details, but it appears the resistance had inside help. The leak came from—"

"I don't care where it came from!" Botha interrupted. "I want to know how we're going to contain this mess!"

Foreign Minister Pik Botha cleared his throat. "Sir, I'm afraid containment may no longer be possible. The international community is in an uproar. We're facing calls for immediate sanctions, even threats of intervention."

The room fell silent as the gravity of the situation sank in. Decades of carefully maintained apartheid policies were crumbling before their eyes.

"Perhaps," began a hesitant voice from the back of the room, "it's time we consider some form of... reform?"

All heads turned to the speaker, a younger minister named Frederik de Klerk. Botha's eyes narrowed dangerously.

"Reform? You want us to capitulate to terrorists and communists?"

De Klerk stood his ground. "Mr. President, the world is changing. If we don't adapt, we'll be left behind — or worse, torn apart."

A heated debate erupted, with hardliners calling for even stricter crackdowns while a growing faction argued for negotiation and gradual change.

As the argument raged on, Botha stared out the window at the city below, where he could see smoke rising from protest fires in the distance. For the first time in his long political career, he felt the ground shifting beneath his feet.

"Enough," he said finally, his voice cutting through the chaos. "We will not decide the future of our nation in one night of panic. But make no mistake, gentlemen — change is coming, whether we like it or not. The question is, will we shape that change, or be destroyed by it?"

As the emergency meeting adjourned in the early hours of the morning, the fate of South Africa hung in the balance. The government was in crisis, and the decisions made in the coming days would determine the course of history for millions.

THE SUN ROSE OVER PORT Elizabeth, casting a golden glow on streets already teeming with people. What had started as scattered protests the night before had swelled into a massive, diverse crowd that stretched as far as the eye could see.

James and Amahle stood at the front of the gathering, their hearts pounding with a mixture of exhilaration and apprehension. They exchanged a glance, years of shared struggle passing between them in an instant.

"Are you ready?" James asked, his voice barely audible above the growing chants.

Amahle nodded, her jaw set with determination. "It's now or never."

As they began to march, the crowd moved as one, a sea of humanity flowing through the city streets. People of all races walked side by side, their voices rising in unified demands for justice and equality.

At the government buildings, lines of riot police stood at the ready, their faces grim behind plastic shields. As the protesters approached, tension crackled in the air.

Suddenly, a young police officer stepped forward, removing his helmet. His hands shook as he lowered his baton. "I... I can't do this," he said, his voice carrying in the sudden hush. "This isn't right."

A ripple passed through the police line. One by one, officers began to lower their weapons. Some stepped aside, while others joined the protesters, their uniforms a stark contrast to the civilian clothes around them.

The crowd's cheers were deafening. James felt tears pricking his eyes as he watched barriers—both literal and figurative—crumble before him.

As the day wore on, similar scenes played out across South Africa. In Cape Town, Johannesburg, and Durban, protests swelled to unprecedented sizes. News broadcasts showed images of white and black South Africans embracing, their shared hopes for a better future transcending decades of enforced separation.

By nightfall, it was clear that a fundamental shift had occurred. The government's control was slipping, and the tide of change was becoming unstoppable.

Back in Port Elizabeth, James and Amahle stood on a makeshift platform, addressing the crowd that had gathered in the city's main square.

"Today," Amahle called out, her voice strong and clear, "we have shown the power of unity. This is only the beginning, but together, we will build a new South Africa!"

As the crowd erupted in cheers, James squeezed Amahle's hand. They both knew that challenges lay ahead, but for the first time in their long struggle, the dawn of a new era seemed truly within reach.

THE FIRST RAYS OF SUNLIGHT crept over the horizon, painting the sky in hues of pink and gold. On a hill overlooking Port Elizabeth, a diverse group of South Africans gathered, their faces etched with a mixture of exhaustion and hope.

James and Amahle stood hand in hand, watching as people from all walks of life - former resistance fighters, reformed government officials, township residents, and suburban families - came together in a circle.

Minister Venter, his suit rumpled from days of nonstop negotiations, cleared his throat. "My fellow South Africans, today we stand at the threshold of a new era. The government has agreed to begin formal negotiations for the dismantling of apartheid and the transition to a democratic system."

A murmur rippled through the crowd, a mix of disbelief and cautious optimism.

Sipho stepped forward, his voice carrying across the gathering. "This is a victory, but our work is far from over. We must remain vigilant and united as we build the future we've fought so hard for."

As the sun climbed higher, casting long shadows across the landscape, people began to share their hopes and fears for the future. Voices that had long been silenced now rang out with dreams of education, opportunity, and reconciliation.

Amahle squeezed James's hand, her voice soft but filled with emotion. "Can you believe we're actually here? After everything we've been through?"

James shook his head, a smile playing at the corners of his mouth. "It feels like a dream. But look around - this is real. We're witnessing the birth of a new South Africa."

As the impromptu gathering began to disperse, people lingered, forming small groups and engaging in conversations that would have been unthinkable just days before. A young white child shyly offered a flower to an elderly black woman, who accepted it with tears in her eyes.

James and Amahle remained on the hilltop, watching as the city below began to stir to life. The road ahead was uncertain, filled with challenges and the hard work of rebuilding a nation. But as the new day dawned, bringing with it the promise of change, they felt a profound sense of hope.

"Whatever comes next," Amahle said, leaning her head on James's shoulder, "we'll face it together. Not just you and me, but all of us."

James nodded, his gaze fixed on the horizon. "Together," he echoed. "For a free and equal South Africa."

As the sun rose fully, bathing the landscape in warm light, it seemed to herald not just a new day, but a new chapter in the nation's history. The dawn of change had finally arrived, and with it, the promise of a brighter future for all South Africans.

Don't miss out!

Visit the website below and you can sign up to receive emails whenever GPTApplied Creative Writing Group publishes a new book. There's no charge and no obligation.

https://books2read.com/r/B-A-DIJSB-VGWPD

BOOKS 2 READ

Connecting independent readers to independent writers.

About the Author

The GPTApplied Creative Writing Group is a collective of innovative storytellers and technologists dedicated to pushing the boundaries of narrative creation. Combining human creativity with cutting-edge artificial intelligence, the group explores new frontiers in literature, crafting compelling stories across a wide range of genres and subjects.

With a diverse background spanning multiple disciplines, the team brings a unique perspective to their work. They are passionate about using their skills to create engaging narratives on various topics, from historical events and social issues to futuristic scenarios and fantastical worlds.

The group is committed to harnessing the power of AI to enhance storytelling, believing in its potential to open up new avenues of creativity and expression. Their work aims to captivate readers while showcasing the exciting possibilities at the intersection of human imagination and artificial intelligence.

Read more at www.gptapplied.com.

About the Publisher

GPTApplied Press is an independent publishing house at the forefront of the AI-assisted content creation revolution. Founded with the vision of harnessing the power of artificial intelligence to enhance human creativity, GPTApplied Press is committed to producing high-quality, innovative works across a wide spectrum of genres and formats.

Our mission is to explore the intersection of technology and content creation, pushing the boundaries of what's possible in modern publishing. We believe in the potential of AI to amplify human creativity, not replace it, resulting in unique and compelling works that speak to contemporary audiences.

GPTApplied Press publishes a diverse range of content, from novels and short stories to textbooks and educational materials. We are dedicated to fostering new voices, tackling important topics, and reimagining the future of publishing across all fields of knowledge.

With a focus on innovation and quality, we aim to publish books that not only inform and entertain but also provoke thought and inspire change. GPTApplied Press is committed to being at the cutting edge of the evolving landscape of AI-assisted publishing, continually exploring new ways to create valuable content for readers and learners worldwide.

www.ingramcontent.com/pod-product-compliance
Lightning Source LLC
Chambersburg PA
CBHW031737150726
47989CB00006B/2497